DOVER · THRIFT · EDITIONS

Tales of Conjure
and the Color Line

10 Stories

CHARLES WADDELL CHESNUTT

Edited and with an Introduction by
JOAN R. SHERMAN

DOVER PUBLICATIONS, INC.
Mineola, New York

DOVER THRIFT EDITIONS

GENERAL EDITOR: PAUL NEGRI

Copyright

Introduction copyright © 1998 by Dover Publications, Inc.
All rights reserved under Pan American and International Copyright Conventions.

Bibliographical Note

Tales of Conjure and the Color Line is a new selection of stories reprinted from standard editions. The introduction has been specially prepared for this edition.

Library of Congress Cataloging-in-Publication Data

Chesnutt, Charles Waddell, 1858–1932.
    Tales of conjure and the color line / Charles W. Chesnutt ; edited and with an introduction by Joan R. Sherman.
        p.   cm.
    ISBN 0-486-40426-9 (pbk.)
    1. Southern States—Social life and customs—Fiction.   2. Racially mixed people—Southern States—Fiction.   3. Afro-Americans—Southern States—Fiction.   I. Sherman, Joan R.   II. Title.
PS1292.C6A6   1998
813'.4—dc21   98-35058
                                                                                         CIP

Manufactured in the United States of America
Dover Publications, Inc., 31 East 2nd Street, Mineola, N.Y. 11501

Introduction

> The saddest spectacle in history is that of warring races upon the same territory, and if the American people can fuse out of the diverse races which now inhabit this continent a really free people, among whom every individual, regardless of anything but his talents and his citizenship, shall find open to him every worthy career for which he may demonstrate his fitness, it will in my opinion have achieved very nearly the ultimate problem of civilization.

Chesnutt expressed this hope for racial harmony and equality almost a century ago, in 1903, and he would no doubt be saddened to find America still far from solving its' "ultimate problem." A professional stenographer, journalist, creative writer, and attorney, Chesnutt was peculiarly sensitive to racial tensions because with only one-sixteenth "Negro blood," he could have passed for white but chose to identify with the black race.

He was born on June 20, 1858, in Cleveland, Ohio, the son of free mulattoes, Andrew Jackson Chesnutt and Ann Maria Sampson. After the Civil War, the family moved to Fayetteville, in the Cape Fear River area of North Carolina, which became the setting for most of Chesnutt's stories of the South. Here his paternal grandfather, Waddell Cade, a wealthy white merchant, helped his father establish a grocery store in which the boy worked while he attended Howard School. Chesnutt was such an outstanding student that at age sixteen he became an instructor at Howard School, and in the next few years he taught in Charlotte and in rural schoolhouses. In 1877, he was assistant principal, and in 1879 principal of the new State Colored Normal School for teacher-training. His formal education had ended in his teens, but Chesnutt pursued lifelong self-education: he read world literature, history, and philosophy; taught himself to play the piano and organ; and learned Latin, Greek, and several European languages.

Chesnutt married Susan U. Perry, a well-educated mulatto, in 1878, and they had three children. Although he was active in church and community affairs, Chesnutt felt estranged from the African Americans of Fayetteville, both the uneducated rural class and the city folk who lacked cultivation. Moreover, although he looked white—"I am really seven-eighths white," he wrote in 1896—Chesnutt lived as one of "the colored people," thereby forfeiting the friendship of the "better class" of white Southerners he so admired.

In 1883, at age 25, Chesnutt moved North; as he had vowed many years before, he would now "see if it's possible for talent, wealth, genius to acquire social standing and distinction" in the North. To these egotistical motives, he added others: by becoming a famous writer, he would benefit his family, his race, and all humanity. Chesnutt's literary goal was to effect a "moral revolution," the elevation of *white* people beyond the "unjust spirit of caste" that subjected his race "to scorn and social ostracism."

> "The Negro's part is to prepare himself for recognition and equality, and it is the province of literature to open the way for him to get it—to accustom the public mind to the idea; to lead people on, imperceptibly, unconsciously, step by step, to the desired state of feeling. If I can do anything to further this work, and can see any likelihood of obtaining success in it, I would gladly devote my life to it." [Journals, May 8, 1880]

Chesnutt's career in literature did not take off very soon nor did it last very long because he could not restrain his anger at racial injustice to "lead people on, imperceptibly." He was a reporter in New York City for a few months and in 1884 moved to Cleveland, Ohio, where he worked as a bookkeeper and a stenographer, while studying law; he passed the Ohio bar in 1887. Chesnutt set up a legal stenographic business in Cleveland which prospered and, together with slim earnings from literature and law, kept his family in upper-middle-class comfort. The Chesnutts owned their own home as well as investments in land and securities; they sent daughters Ethel and Helen to Smith College and son Edwin to Harvard; they enjoyed domestic help at home and rented cottages in the summer; and they belonged to exclusive clubs— the Cleveland Social Circle, the Tresart and Rowfant Clubs—whose snobbery Chesnutt satirized in his stories.

In the early 1880s, periodicals published some of Chesnutt's stories and sketches, but his first real success came in August, 1887, when "The Goophered Grapevine" appeared in the *Atlantic Monthly*. He vigorously pursued literary fame and fortune from 1889 to 1905. During that period notable publishers brought out his two collections of stories, a biography, and three novels. To promote his fiction, Chesnutt gave readings and lectures; he wrote continually to publishers, editors, politicians, and friends about the advertising, sales, and reviews of his books; he sought editorial and publishing advice from luminaries of the white literary establishment, including George Washington Cable, Albion W. Tourgee, Walter Hines Page, and William Dean Howells, America's foremost literary critic. A high point of Chesnutt's career was Howells' review of his two story collections. Howells admired the "novelty of the material," the writer's "quiet self-restraint" and detachment, and his artistry comparable to that of Henry James and Sarah Orne Jewett. "He sees his people very clearly, very justly, and he shows them as he sees them, . . . He touches all the stops, and with equal delicacy in stories of real tragedy and comedy and pathos. . . . He has sounded a fresh note, boldly, not blatantly, and he has won the ear of the more intelligent public." (*Atlantic Monthly*, 85 [May 1900], 699–701). Unhappily, the "more intelligent public" were few indeed: *The Conjure Woman* sold only 1,500 copies. Disappointed but undefeated, Chesnutt went on to write three novels, but as these moved increasingly further away from art toward polemic, he lost his audience.

Racial equality and advancement were never far from Chesnutt's mind in this period, as seen in his essays and his letters to African American leaders like Booker T. Washington, W. E. B. DuBois, T. Thomas Fortune, and William M. Trotter. Before 1901, Chesnutt largely subsumed racial protest to the art of fiction. In his "conjure" stories of the 1880s, congenial humor, ironic wit, and clever framing subtly disguise the serious racial messages; indeed, artful manipulation is the name of the game in these tales where at least three levels of conjurers operate: Chesnutt, inventor and chief shaman; Uncle Julius, the crafty narrator, enchanting white John and Annie; Aun' Peggy, the "witch," and assorted tricksters among the blacks, casting their magical spells, manipulating people and nature. In stories of the color line, too, Chesnutt impressed readers with his psychological insights and vivid portrayals of fully humanized mixed-race characters, although many readers objected to the fictions' racial politics. Chesnutt's novels were admired principally by black readers but failed to win widespread critical or popular acclaim: *The House Behind the Cedars* sold only 3,244 copies by 1904; *The Marrow of Tradition*, his most popular novel, sold 3,276 copies in 1901, 111 in 1902, and none in 1903. White readers, Chesnutt's chosen target, rejected the strident militancy of the novelist's voice, now furious at the South's betrayals, bitter over his own failure to surmount the "color line in literature," angry at a world lacking social justice for African Americans. Chesnutt's rage emerged clearly in his letters of 1901–1905: for example, writing to Booker T. Washington, he denounced Southern restrictions on black suffrage and said: "I have no confidence in that friendship of the whites which is to take the place of rights, and no expectation of justice at their hands unless it is founded on law. . . . If the white South will continue to ignore the Constitution and violate the laws, it must be with no consent of mine, . . . " (June 27, 1903) Again, firmly rejecting Washington's conciliatory attitudes, Chesnutt insisted: "I want my rights, and all of them, . . . And I do not believe in a silent submission to any form of injustice." (August 11, 1903)

After the failure of his final novel in 1905, Chesnutt abandoned the "dream" of his life—"to be an author" (1881). His political activism continued as he championed the accomplishments and rights of African Americans in articles and lectures and with national organizations until his death in 1932. Among the honors Chesnutt received were an LL.D. degree from Wilberforce University in 1913; election to the National Arts Club in 1917; and in 1928, the NAACP Spingarn Medal for his "pioneer work as a literary artist depicting the life and struggles of Americans of Negro descent."

Although literary fame and fortune eluded him in life, since the late 1960s Chesnutt has earned high praise for his masterful, innovative stories. Among African Americans writers, he was the first to weave black folklore and realistic folk life, myths, superstitions, and tragic racial conflicts into vibrant tales of the Old and New South. He was the first to realistically portray middle-class mixed-blood men and women, their values, manners, and problems. Chesnutt's fictional range was wide: he bared the plight of the disadvantaged lower classes, both black and white; he revealed the shared humanity of people of all classes and races; he decried and satirized economic, social, and political discrimination against minorities in America. Among his contemporary fiction writers, Chesnutt stands tall as a fine and forceful stylist who admirably handled dialects, rhetorical figures, symbolic imagery, and a wide range of non-stereotypical characters; and he is important as a local colorist who surely captured the sights, sounds, and customs of both southern and northern African American communities. Chesnutt was the father of the African American short story and an inspiring force for the writers of the Harlem Renaissance.

JOAN R. SHERMAN

Contents

THE GOOPHERED GRAPEVINE

SOME YEARS ago my wife was in poor health, and our family doctor, in whose skill and honesty I had implicit confidence, advised a change of climate. I shared, from an unprofessional standpoint, his opinion that the raw winds, the chill rains, and the violent changes of temperature that characterized the winters in the region of the Great Lakes tended to aggravate my wife's difficulty, and would undoubtedly shorten her life if she remained exposed to them. The doctor's advice was that we seek, not a temporary place of sojourn, but a permanent residence, in a warmer and more equable climate. I was engaged at the time in grape-culture in northern Ohio, and, as I liked the business and had given it much study, I decided to look for some other locality suitable for carrying it on. I thought of sunny France, of sleepy Spain, of Southern California, but there were objections to them all. It occurred to me that I might find what I wanted in some one of our own Southern States. It was a sufficient time after the war for conditions in the South to have become somewhat settled; and I was enough of a pioneer to start a new industry, if I could not find a place where grape-culture had been tried. I wrote to a cousin who had gone into the turpentine business in central North Carolina. He assured me, in response to my inquiries, that no better place could be found in the South than the State and neighborhood where he lived; the climate was perfect for health, and, in conjunction with the soil, ideal for grape-culture; labor was cheap, and land could be bought for a mere song. He gave us a cordial invitation to come and visit him while we looked into the matter. We accepted the invitation, and after several days of leisurely travel, the last hundred miles of which were up a river on a sidewheel steamer, we reached our destination, a quaint old town, which I shall call Patesville, because, for one reason, that is not its name. There was a red brick market-house in the public square, with a tall tower, which held a four-faced clock that struck the hours, and from which there pealed out a

1

curfew at nine o'clock. There were two or three hotels, a court-house, a jail, stores, offices, and all the appurtenances of a county seat and a commercial emporium; for while Patesville numbered only four or five thousand inhabitants, of all shades of complexion, it was one of the principal towns in North Carolina, and had a considerable trade in cotton and naval stores. This business activity was not immediately apparent to my unaccustomed eyes. Indeed, when I first saw the town, there brooded over it a calm that seemed almost sabbatic in its restfulness, though I learned later on that underneath its somnolent exterior the deeper currents of life—love and hatred, joy and despair, ambition and avarice, faith and friendship—flowed not less steadily than in livelier latitudes.

We found the weather delightful at that season, the end of summer, and were hospitably entertained. Our host was a man of means and evidently regarded our visit as a pleasure, and we were therefore correspondingly at our ease, and in a position to act with the coolness of judgment desirable in making so radical a change in our lives. My cousin placed a horse and buggy at our disposal, and himself acted as our guide until I became somewhat familiar with the country.

I found that grape-culture, while it had never been carried on to any great extent, was not entirely unknown in the neighborhood. Several planters thereabouts had attempted it on a commercial scale, in former years, with greater or less success; but like most Southern industries, it had felt the blight of war and had fallen into desuetude.

I went several times to look at a place that I thought might suit me. It was a plantation of considerable extent, that had formerly belonged to a wealthy man by the name of McAdoo. The estate had been for years involved in litigation between disputing heirs, during which period shiftless cultivation had well-nigh exhausted the soil. There had been a vineyard of some extent on the place, but it had not been attended to since the war, and had lapsed into utter neglect. The vines—here partly supported by decayed and broken-down trellises, there twining themselves among the branches of the slender saplings which had sprung up among them—grew in wild and unpruned luxuriance, and the few scattered grapes they bore were the undisputed prey of the first comer. The site was admirably adapted to grape-raising; the soil, with a little attention, could not have been better; and with the native grape, the luscious scuppernong, as my main reliance in the beginning, I felt sure that I could introduce and cultivate successfully a number of other varieties.

One day I went over with my wife to show her the place. We drove out of the town over a long wooden bridge that spanned a spreading mill-pond, passed the long whitewashed fence surrounding the county fair-ground, and struck into a road so sandy that the horse's feet sank to the fetlocks. Our route lay partly up hill and partly down, for we were in the sand-hill country; we drove past cultivated farms, and then by abandoned fields grown up in scrub-oak and short-leaved pine, and once or twice through the solemn aisles of the virgin forest, where the tall pines, well-nigh meeting over the narrow road, shut out the sun, and wrapped us in cloistral solitude. Once, at a crossroads, I was in doubt as to the turn to take, and we sat there waiting ten minutes—we had already caught some of the native infection of restfulness—for some human being to come along, who could direct us on our way. At length a little negro girl appeared, walking straight as an arrow, with a piggin full of water on her head. After a little patient investigation, necessary to overcome the child's shyness, we learned what we wished to know, and at the end of about five miles from the town reached our destination.

We drove between a pair of decayed gateposts—the gate itself had long since disappeared—and up a straight sandy lane, between two lines of rotting rail fence, partly concealed by jimson-weeds and briers, to the open space where a dwelling-house had once stood, evidently a spacious mansion, if we might judge from the ruined chimneys that were still standing, and the brick pillars on which the sills rested. The house itself, we had been informed, had fallen a victim to the fortunes of war.

We alighted from the buggy, walked about the yard for a while, and then wandered off into the adjoining vineyard. Upon Annie's complaining of weariness I led the way back to the yard, where a pine log, lying under a spreading elm, afforded a shady though somewhat hard seat. One end of the log was already occupied by a venerable-looking colored man. He held on his knees a hat full of grapes, over which he was smacking his lips with great gusto, and a pile of grapeskins near him indicated that the performance was no new thing. We approached him at an angle from the rear, and were close to him before he perceived us. He respectfully rose as we drew near, and was moving away, when I begged him to keep his seat.

"Don't let us disturb you," I said. "There is plenty of room for us all."

He resumed his seat with somewhat of embarrassment. While he had been standing, I had observed that he was a tall man, and, though slightly bowed by the weight of years, apparently quite vigorous. He was not entirely black, and this fact, together with the quality of his hair, which was about six inches long and very bushy, except on the top of his head, where he was quite bald, suggested a slight strain of other than negro blood. There was a shrewdness in his eyes, too, which was not altogether African, and which, as we afterward learned from experience, was indicative of a corresponding shrewdness in his character. He went on eating the grapes, but did not seem to enjoy himself quite so well as he had apparently done before he became aware of our presence.

"Do you live around here?" I asked, anxious to put him at his ease.

"Yas, suh. I lives des ober yander, behine de nex' san'-hill, on de Lumberton plank-road."

"Do you know anything about the time when this vineyard was cultivated?"

"Lawd bless you, suh, I knows all about it. Dey ain' na'er a man in dis settlement w'at won' tell you ole Julius McAdoo 'uz bawn en raise' on dis yer same plantation. Is you de Norv'n gemman w'at's gwine ter buy de ole vimya'd?"

"I am looking at it," I replied; "but I don't know that I shall care to buy unless I can be reasonably sure of making something out of it."

"Well, suh, you is a stranger ter me, en I is a stranger ter you, en we is bofe strangers ter one anudder, but 'f I 'uz in yo' place, I wouldn' buy dis vimya'd."

"Why not?" I asked.

"Well, I dunno whe'r you b'lieves in cunj'in' er not,—some er de w'ite folks don't, er says dey don't,—but de truf er de matter is dat dis yer ole vimya'd is goophered."

"Is what?" I asked, not grasping the meaning of this unfamiliar word.

"Is goophered,—cunju'd, bewitch'."

He imparted this information with such solemn earnestness, and with such an air of confidential mystery, that I felt somewhat interested, while Annie was evidently much impressed, and drew closer to me.

"How do you know it is bewitched?" I asked.

"I wouldn' spec' fer you ter b'lieve me 'less you know all 'bout de fac's. But ef you en young miss dere doan' min' lis'nin' ter a ole nigger run on a minute er two w'ile you er restin', I kin 'splain to you how it all happen'."

We assured him that we would be glad to hear how it all happened, and he began to tell us. At first the current of his memory—or imagination—seemed somewhat sluggish; but as his embarrassment wore off, his language flowed more freely, and the story acquired perspective and coherence. As he became more and more absorbed in the narrative, his eyes assumed a dreamy expression, and he seemed to lose sight of his auditors, and to be living over again in monologue his life on the old plantation.

"Ole Mars Dugal' McAdoo," he began, "bought dis place long many years befo' de wah, en I 'member well w'en he sot out all dis yer part er de plantation in scuppernon's. De vimes growed monst'us fas', en Mars Dugal' made a thousan' gallon er scuppernon' wine eve'y year.

"Now, ef dey's an'thing a nigger lub, nex' ter 'possum, en chick'n, en watermillyums, it's scuppernon's. Dey ain' nuffin dat kin stan' up side'n de scuppernon' fer sweetness; sugar ain't a suckumstance ter scuppernon'. W'en de season is nigh 'bout ober, en de grapes begin ter swivel up des a little wid de wrinkles er ole age,—w'en de skin git sof' en brown,—den de scuppernon' make you smack yo' lip en roll yo' eye en wush fer mo'; so I reckon it ain' very 'stonishin' dat niggers lub scuppernon'.

"Dey wuz a sight er niggers in de naberhood er de vimya'd. Dere wuz ole Mars Henry Brayboy's niggers, en ole Mars Jeems McLean's niggers, en Mars Dugal's own niggers; den dey wuz a settlement er free niggers en po' buckrahs down by de Wim'l'ton Road, en Mars Dugal' had de only vimya'd in de naberhood. I reckon it ain' so much so nowadays, but befo' de wah, in slab'ry times, a nigger didn' mine goin' fi' er ten mile in a night, w'en dey wuz sump'n good ter eat at de yuther een'.

"So atter a w'ile Mars Dugal' begin ter miss his scuppernon's. Co'se he 'cuse' de niggers er it, but dey all 'nied it ter de las'. Mars Dugal' sot spring guns en steel traps, en he en de oberseah sot up nights once't er twice't, tel one night Mars Dugal'—he 'uz a monst'us keerless man—got his leg shot full er cow-peas. But somehow er nudder dey couldn' nebber ketch none er de niggers. I dunner how it happen, but it happen des like I tell you, en de grapes kep' on a-goin' des de same.

"But bimeby ole Mars Dugal' fix' up a plan ter stop it. Dey wuz a cunjuh 'oman livin' down 'mongs' de free niggers on de Wim'l'ton Road, en all de darkies fum Rockfish ter Beaver Crick wuz feared er her. She could wuk de mos' powerfulles' kin' er goopher,—could make people hab fits, er rheumatiz, er make 'em des dwinel away en die; en dey say she went out ridin' de niggers at night, fer she wuz a witch 'sides bein' a cunjuh 'oman. Mars Dugal' hearn 'bout Aun' Peggy's doin's, en begun ter 'flect whe'r er no he couldn' git her ter he'p him keep de niggers off'n de grapevimes. One day in de spring er de year, ole miss pack' up a basket er chick'n en poun'-cake, en a bottle er scuppernon' wine, en Mars Dugal' tuk it in his buggy en driv ober ter Aun' Peggy's cabin. He tuk de basket in, en had a long talk wid Aun' Peggy.

"De nex' day Aun' Peggy come up ter de vimya'd. De niggers seed her slippin' 'roun', en dey soon foun' out what she 'uz doin' dere. Mars Dugal' had hi'ed her ter goopher de grapevimes. She sa'ntered 'roun' 'mongs' de vimes, en tuk a leaf fum dis one, en a grape-hull fum dat one, en a grape-seed fum anudder one; en den a little twig fum here, en a little pinch er dirt fum dere,—en put it all in a big black bottle, wid a snake's toof en a speckle' hen's gall en some ha'rs fum a black cat's tail, en den fill' de bottle wid scuppernon' wine. W'en she got de goopher all ready en fix', she tuk 'n went out in de woods en buried it under de root uv a red oak tree, en den come back en tole one er de niggers she done goopher de grapevimes, en a'er a nigger w'at eat dem grapes 'ud be sho ter die inside'n twel' mont's.

"Atter dat de niggers let de scuppernon's 'lone, en Mars Dugal' didn' hab no 'casion ter fine no mo' fault; en de season wuz mos' gone, w'en a strange gemman stop at de plantation one night ter see Mars Dugal' on some business; en his coachman, seein' de scuppernon's growin' so nice en sweet, slip 'roun' behine de smoke-house, en et all de scuppernon's he could hole. Nobody didn' notice it at de time, but dat night, on de way home, de gemman's hoss runned away en kill' de coachman. W'en we hearn de noos, Aun' Lucy, de cook, she up 'n say she seed de strange nigger eat'n' er de scuppernon's behine de smoke-house; en den we knowed de goopher had b'en er wukkin'. Den one er de nigger chilluns runned away fum de quarters one day, en got in de scuppernon's, en died de nex' week. W'ite folks say he die' er de fevuh, but de niggers knowed it wuz de goopher. So you k'n be sho de darkies didn' hab much ter do wid dem scuppernon' vimes.

"W'en de scuppernon' season 'uz ober fer dat year, Mars Dugal' foun' he had made fifteen hund'ed gallon er wine; en one er de niggers hearn him laffin' wid de oberseah fit ter kill, en sayin' dem fifteen hund'ed gallon er wine wuz monst'us good intrus' on de ten dollars he laid out on de vimya'd. So I 'low ez he paid Aun' Peggy ten dollars fer to goopher de grapevimes.

"De goopher didn' wuk no mo' tel de nex' summer, w'en 'long to'ds de middle er de season one er de fiel' han's died; en ez dat lef' Mars Dugal' sho't er han's, he went off ter town fer ter buy anudder. He fotch de noo nigger home wid 'im. He wuz er ole nigger, er de color er a gingy-cake, en ball ez a hoss-apple on de top er his head. He wuz a peart ole nigger, do', en could do a big day's wuk.

"Now it happen dat one er de niggers on de nex' plantation, one er ole Mars Henry Brayboy's niggers, had runned away de day befo', en tuk ter de swamp, en ole Mars Dugal' en some er de yuther nabor w'ite folks had gone out wid dere guns en dere dogs fer ter he'p 'em hunt fer de nigger; en de han's on our own plantation wuz all so flusterated dat we fuhgot ter tell de noo han' 'bout de goopher on de scuppernon' vimes. Co'se he smell de grapes en see de vimes, an atter dahk de fus' thing he done wuz ter slip off ter de grapevimes 'dout sayin' nuffin ter nobody. Nex' mawnin' he tole some er de niggers 'bout de fine bait er scuppernon' he et de night befo'.

"W'en dey tole 'im 'bout de goopher on de grapevimes, he 'uz dat tarrified dat he turn pale, en look des like he gwine ter die right in his tracks. De oberseah come up en axed w'at 'uz de matter; en w'en dey tole 'im Henry be'n eatin' er de scuppernon's, en got de goopher on 'im, he gin Henry a big drink er w'iskey, en 'low dat de nex' rainy day he take 'im ober ter Aun' Peggy's, en see ef she wouldn' take de goopher off'n him, seein' ez he didn' know nuffin erbout it tel he done et de grapes.

"Sho nuff, it rain de nex' day, en de oberseah went ober ter Aun' Peggy's wid Henry. En Aun' Peggy say dat bein' ez Henry didn' know 'bout de goopher, en et de grapes in ign'ance er de conseq'ences, she reckon she mought be able fer ter take de goopher off'n him. So she fotch out er bottle wid some conjuh medicine in it, en po'd some out in a go'd fer Henry ter drink. He manage ter git it down: he say it tas'e like whiskey wid sump'n bitter in it. She 'lowed dat 'ud keep de goopher off'n him tel de spring; but w'en de sap begin ter rise in de grapevimes he ha' ter come en see her ag'in, en she tell him w'at e's ter do.

"Nex' spring, w'en de sap commence' ter rise in de scuppernon' vime, Henry tuk a ham one night. Whar'd he git de ham? I doan know; dey wa'n't no hams on de plantation 'cep'n' w'at 'uz in de smoke-house, but I never see Henry 'bout de smoke-house. But ez I wuz a-sayin', he tuk de ham ober ter Aun' Peggy's; en Aun' Peggy tole 'im dat w'en Mars Dugal' begin ter prune de grapevimes, he mus' go en take 'n scrape off de sap whar it ooze out'n de cut een's er de vimes, en 'n'int his ball head wid it; en ef he do dat once't a year de goopher wouldn' wuk again 'im long ez he done it. En bein' ez he fotch her de ham, she fix' it so he kin eat all de scuppernon' he want.

"So Henry 'n'int his head wid de sap out'n de big grapevime des ha'f way 'twix' de quarters en de big house, en de goopher nebber wuk agin him dat summer. But de beatenes' thing you eber see happen ter Henry. Up ter dat time he wuz ez ball ez a sweeten' 'tater, but des ez soon ez de young leaves begun ter come out on de grapevimes, de ha'r begun ter grow out on Henry's head, en by de middle er de summer he had de bigges' head er ha'r on de plantation. Befo' dat, Henry had tol'able good ha'r 'roun' de aidges, but soon ez de young grapes begun ter come, Henry's ha'r begun to quirl all up in little balls, des like dis yer reg'lar grapy ha'r, en by de time de grapes got ripe his head look des like a bunch er grapes. Combin' it didn' do no good; he wuk at it ha'f de night wid er Jim Crow,[1] en think he git it straighten' out, but in de mawnin' de grapes 'ud be dere des de same. So he gin it up, en tried ter keep de grapes down by havin' his ha'r cut sho't.

---

[1] A small card, resembling a currycomb in construction, and used by negroes in the rural districts instead of a comb.

"But dat wa'n't de quares' thing 'bout de goopher. When Henry come ter de plantation, he wuz gittin' a little ole an stiff in de j'ints. But dat summer he got des ez spry en libely ez any young nigger on de plantation; fac', he got so biggity dat Mars Jackson, de oberseah, ha' ter th'eaten ter whip 'im, ef he didn' stop cuttin' up his didos en behave hisse'f. But de mos' cur'ouses' thing happen' in de fall, when de sap begin ter go down in de grapevimes. Fus', when de grapes 'uz gethered, de knots begun ter straighten out'n Henry's ha'r; en w'en de leaves begin ter fall, Henry's ha'r 'mence' ter drap out; en when de vimes 'uz bar', Henry's head wuz baller 'n it wuz in de spring, en he begin ter get ole en stiff in de j'ints ag'in, en paid no mo' 'tention ter de gals dyoin' er de whole winter. En nex' spring, w'en he rub de sap on ag'in, he got young ag'in, en so soopl en libely dat none er de young niggers on de plantation couldn' jump, ner dance, ner hoe ez much cotton ez Henry. But in de fall er de year his grapes 'mence' ter straighten out, en his j'ints ter git stiff, en his ha'r drap off, en de rheumatiz begin ter wrastle wid 'im.

"Now, ef you'd 'a' knowed ole Mars Dugal' McAdoo, you'd 'a' knowed dat it ha' ter be a mighty rainy day when he couldn' fine sump'n fer his niggers ter do, en it ha' ter be a mighty little hole he couldn' craw thoo, en ha' ter be a monst'us cloudy night when a dollar git by him in de dahkness; en w'en he see how Henry git young in de spring en ole in de fall, he 'lowed ter hisse'f ez how he could make mo' money out'n Henry dan by wukkin' him in de cotton-fiel'. 'Long de nex' spring, atter de sap 'mence' ter rise, en Henry 'n'int 'is head en sta'ted fer ter git young en soopl, Mars Dugal' up 'n tuk Henry ter town, en sole 'im fer fifteen hunder' dollars. Co'se de man w'at bought Henry didn' know nuffin 'bout de goopher, en Mars Dugal' didn' see no 'casion fer ter tell 'im. Long to'ds de fall, w'en de sap went down, Henry begin ter git ole ag'in same ez yuzhal, en his noo marster begin ter git skeered les'n he gwine ter lose his fifteen-hunder'-dollar nigger. He sent fer a mighty fine doctor, but de med'cine didn' 'pear ter do no good; de goopher had a good holt. Henry tole de doctor 'bout de goopher, but de doctor des laff at 'im.

"One day in de winter Mars Dugal' went ter town, en wuz santerin' 'long de Main Street, when who should he meet but Henry's noo marster. Dey said 'Hoddy,' en Mars Dugal' ax 'im ter hab a seegyar; en atter dey run on awhile 'bout de craps en de weather, Mars Dugal' ax 'im, sorter keerless, like ez ef he des thought of it,—

"'How you like de nigger I sole you las' spring?'

"Henry's marster shuck his head en knock de ashes off'n his seegyar.

"'Spec' I made a bad bahgin when I bought dat nigger. Henry done good wuk all de summer, but sence de fall set in he 'pears ter be sorter

pinin' away. Dey ain' nuffin pertickler de matter wid 'im—leastways de
doctor say so—'cep'n' a tech er de rheumatiz; but his ha'r is all fell out,
en ef he don't pick up his strenk mighty soon, I spec' I'm gwine ter
lose 'im.'

"Dey smoked on awhile, en bimeby ole mars say, 'Well, a bahgin's a
bahgin, but you en me is good fren's, en I doan wan' ter see you lose
all de money you paid fer dat nigger; en ef w'at you say is so, en I ain't
'sputin' it, he ain't wuf much now. I 'spec's you wukked him too ha'd
dis summer, er e'se de swamps down here don't agree wid de san'-hill
nigger. So you des lemme know, en ef he gits any wusser I'll be willin'
ter gib yer five hund'ed dollars fer 'im, en take my chances on his livin'.'

"Sho 'nuff, when Henry begun ter draw up wid de rheumatiz en it
look like he gwine ter die fer sho, his noo marster sen' fer Mars Dugal',
en Mars Dugal' gin him what he promus, en brung Henry home ag'in.
He tuk good keer uv 'im dyoin' er de winter,—give 'im w'iskey ter rub
his rheumatiz, en terbacker ter smoke, en all he want ter eat,—'caze a
nigger w'at he could make a thousan' dollars a year off'n didn' grow on
eve'y huckleberry bush.

"Nex' spring, w'en de sap ris en Henry's ha'r commence' ter sprout,
Mars Dugal' sole 'im ag'in, down in Robeson County dis time; en he
kep' dat sellin' business up fer five year er mo'. Henry nebber say nuffin
'bout de goopher ter his noo marsters, 'caze he know he gwine ter be
tuk good keer uv de nex' winter, w'en Mars Dugal' buy him back. En
Mars Dugal' made 'nuff money off'n Henry ter buy anudder plantation
ober on Beaver Crick.

"But 'long 'bout de een' er dat five year dey come a stranger ter stop
at de plantation. De fus' day he 'uz dere he went out wid Mars Dugal'
en spent all de mawnin' lookin' ober de vimya'd, en atter dinner dey
spent all de evenin' playin' kya'ds. De niggers soon 'skiver' dat he wuz
a Yankee, en dat he come down ter Norf C'lina fer ter l'arn de w'ite
folks how to raise grapes en make wine. He promus Mars Dugal' he c'd
make de grapevimes b'ar twice't ez many grapes, en dat de noo wine-
press he wuz a-sellin' would make mo' d'n twice't ez many gallons er
wine. En ole Mars Dugal' des drunk it all in, des 'peared ter be bewitch' wid dat Yankee. W'en de darkies see dat Yankee runnin' 'roun'
de vimya'd en diggin' under de grapevimes, dey shuk dere heads, en
'lowed dat dey feared Mars Dugal' losin' his min'. Mars Dugal' had all
de dirt dug away fum under de roots er all de scuppernon' vimes, an'
let 'em stan' dat away fer a week er mo'. Den dat Yankee made de niggers fix up a mixtry er lime en ashes en manyo, en po' it 'roun' de roots
er de grapevimes. Den he 'vise Mars Dugal' fer ter trim de vimes
close't, en Mars Dugal' tuck 'n done eve'ything de Yankee tole him ter
do. Dyoin' all er dis time, mind yer, dis yer Yankee wuz libbin' off'n de

fat er de lan', at de big house, en playin' kya'ds wid Mars Dugal' eve'y night; en dey say Mars Dugal' los' mo'n a thousan' dollars dyoin' er de week dat Yankee wuz a-ruinin' de grapevimes.

"W'en de sap ris nex' spring, ole Henry 'n'inted his head ez yuzhal, en his ha'r 'mence' ter grow des de same ez it done eve'y year. De scuppernon' vimes growed monst'us fas', en de leaves wuz greener en thicker dan dey eber be'n dyoin' my rememb'ance; en Henry's ha'r growed out thicker dan eber, en he 'peared ter git younger 'n younger, en soopler 'n soopler; en seein' ez he wuz sho't er han's dat spring, havin' tuk in consid'able noo groun', Mars Dugal' 'cluded he wouldn' sell Henry 'tel he git de crap in en de cotton chop'. So he kep' Henry on de plantation.

"But 'long 'bout time fer de grapes ter come on de scuppernon' vimes, dey 'peared ter come a change ober 'em; de leaves withered en swivel' up, en de young grapes turn' yaller, en bimeby eve'ybody on de plantation could see dat de whole vimya'd wuz dyin'. Mars Dugal' tuk 'n water de vimes en done all he could, but 't wa'n' no use: dat Yankee had done bus' de watermillyum. One time de vimes picked up a bit, en Mars Dugal' 'lowed dey wuz gwine ter come out ag'in; but dat Yankee done dug too close under de roots, en prune de branches too close ter de vime, en all dat lime en ashes done burn' de life out'n de vimes, en dey des kep' a-with'in' en a-swivelin'.

"All dis time de goopher wuz a-wukkin'. When de vimes sta'ted ter wither, Henry 'mence' ter complain er his rheumatiz; en when de leaves begin ter dry up, his ha'r 'mence' ter drap out. When de vimes fresh' up a bit, Henry'd git peart ag'in, en when de vimes wither' ag'in, Henry'd git ole ag'in, en des kep' gittin' mo' en mo' fitten fer nuffin; he des pined away, en pined away, en fine'ly tuk ter his cabin; en when de big vime whar he got de sap ter 'n'int his head withered en turned yaller en died, Henry died too,—des went out sorter like a cannel. Dey didn't 'pear ter be nuffin de matter wid 'im, 'cep'n' de rheumatiz, but his strenk des dwinel' away 'tel he didn' hab ernuff lef' ter draw his bref. De goopher had got de under holt, en th'owed Henry dat time fer good en all.

"Mars Dugal' tuk on might'ly 'bout losin' his vimes en his nigger in de same year; en he swo' dat ef he could git holt er dat Yankee he'd wear 'im ter a frazzle, en den chaw up de frazzle; en he'd done it, too, for Mars Dugal' 'uz a monst'us brash man w'en he once git started. He sot de vimya'd out ober ag'in, but it wuz th'ee er fo' year befo' de vimes got ter b'arin' any scuppernon's.

"W'en de wah broke out, Mars Dugal' raise' a comp'ny, en went off ter fight de Yankees. He say he wuz mighty glad dat wah come, en he des want ter kill a Yankee fer eve'y dollar he los' 'long er dat graperaisin' Yankee. En I 'spec' he would 'a' done it, too, ef de Yankees hadn' s'picioned sump'n, en killed him fus'. Atter de s'render ole miss move' ter town, de niggers all scattered 'way fum de plantation, en de vimya'd ain' be'n cultervated sence."

"Is that story true?" asked Annie doubtfully, but seriously, as the old man concluded his narrative.

"It's des ez true ez I'm a-settin' here, miss. Dey's a easy way ter prove it: I kin lead de way right ter Henry's grave ober yander in de plantation buryin'-groun'. En I tell yer w'at, marster, I wouldn' 'vise you to buy dis yer ole vimya'd, 'caze de goopher's on it yit, en dey ain' no tellin' w'en it's gwine ter crap out."

"But I thought you said all the old vines died."

"Dey did 'pear ter die, but a few un 'em come out ag'in, en is mixed in 'mongs' de yuthers. I ain't skeered ter eat de grapes, 'caze I knows de old vimes fum de noo ones; but wid strangers dey ain' no tellin' w'at mought happen. I wouldn' 'vise yer ter buy dis vimya'd."

I bought the vineyard, nevertheless, and it has been for a long time in a thriving condition, and is often referred to by the local press as a striking illustration of the opportunities open to Northern capital in the development of Southern industries. The luscious scuppernong holds first rank among our grapes, though we cultivate a great many other varieties, and our income from grapes packed and shipped to the Northern markets is quite considerable. I have not noticed any developments of the goopher in the vineyard, although I have a mild suspicion that our colored assistants do not suffer from want of grapes during the season.

I found, when I bought the vineyard, that Uncle Julius had occupied a cabin on the place for many years, and derived a respectable revenue from the product of the neglected grapevines. This, doubtless, accounted for his advice to me not to buy the vineyard, though whether it inspired the goopher story I am unable to state. I believe, however, that the wages I paid him for his services as coachman, for I gave him employment in that capacity, were more than an equivalent for anything he lost by the sale of the vineyard.

PO' SANDY

On the northeast corner of my vineyard in central North Carolina, and fronting on the Lumberton plank-road, there stood a small frame house, of the simplest construction. It was built of pine lumber, and contained but one room, to which one window gave light and one door admission. Its weather-beaten sides revealed a virgin innocence of paint. Against one end of the house, and occupying half its width, there stood a huge brick chimney: the crumbling mortar had left large cracks between the bricks; the bricks themselves had begun to scale off in large flakes, leaving the chimney sprinkled with unsightly blotches. These evidences of decay were but partially concealed by a creeping vine, which extended its slender branches hither and thither in an ambitious but futile attempt to cover the whole chimney. The wooden shutter, which had once protected the unglazed window, had fallen from its hinges, and lay rotting in the rank grass and jimson-weeds beneath. This building, I learned when I bought the place, had been used as a schoolhouse for several years prior to the breaking out of the war, since which time it had remained unoccupied, save when some stray cow or vagrant hog had sought shelter within its walls from the chill rains and nipping winds of winter.

One day my wife requested me to build her a new kitchen. The house erected by us, when we first came to live upon the vineyard, contained a very conveniently arranged kitchen; but for some occult reason my wife wanted a kitchen in the back yard, apart from the dwelling-house, after the usual Southern fashion. Of course I had to build it.

To save expense, I decided to tear down the old schoolhouse, and use the lumber, which was in a good state of preservation, in the construction of the new kitchen. Before demolishing the old house, however, I made an estimate of the amount of material contained in it, and found that I would have to buy several hundred feet of lumber additional, in order to build the new kitchen according to my wife's plan.

One morning old Julius McAdoo, our colored coachman, harnessed the gray mare to the rockaway, and drove my wife and me over to the sawmill from which I meant to order the new lumber. We drove down the long lane which led from our house to the plank-road; following the plank-road for about a mile, we turned into a road running through the forest and across the swamp to the sawmill beyond. Our carriage jolted over the half-rotted corduroy road which traversed the swamp, and then climbed the long hill leading to the sawmill. When we reached the mill, the foreman had gone over to a neighboring farmhouse, probably to smoke or gossip, and we were compelled to await his return before we could transact our business. We remained seated in the carriage, a few rods from the mill, and watched the leisurely movements of the mill-hands. We had not waited long before a huge pine log was placed in position, the machinery of the mill was set in motion, and the circular saw began to eat its way through the log, with a loud whir which resounded throughout the vicinity of the mill. The sound rose and fell in a sort of rhythmic cadence, which, heard from where we sat, was not unpleasing, and not loud enough to prevent conversation. When the saw started on its second journey through the log, Julius observed, in a lugubrious tone, and with a perceptible shudder:—

"Ugh! but dat des do cuddle my blood!"

"What's the matter, Uncle Julius?" inquired my wife, who is of a very sympathetic turn of mind. "Does the noise affect your nerves?"

"No, Mis' Annie," replied the old man, with emotion, "I ain' narvous; but dat saw, a-cuttin' en grindin' thoo dat stick er timber, en moanin', en groanin', en sweekin', kyars my 'memb'ance back ter ole times, en 'min's me er po' Sandy." The pathetic intonation with which he lengthened out the "po' Sandy" touched a responsive chord in our own hearts.

"And who was poor Sandy?" asked my wife, who takes a deep interest in the stories of plantation life which she hears from the lips of the older colored people. Some of these stories are quaintly humorous; others wildly extravagant, revealing the Oriental cast of the negro's imagination; while others, poured freely into the sympathetic ear of a Northern-bred woman, disclose many a tragic incident of the darker side of slavery.

"Sandy," said Julius, in reply to my wife's question, "was a nigger w'at useter b'long ter ole Mars Marrabo McSwayne. Mars Marrabo's place wuz on de yuther side'n de swamp, right nex' ter yo' place. Sandy wuz a monst'us good nigger, en could do so many things erbout a plantation, en alluz 'ten' ter his wuk so well, dat w'en Mars Marrabo's chilluns growed up en married off, dey all un 'em wanted dey daddy fer ter gin 'em Sandy fer a weddin' present. But Mars Marrabo knowed de res' wouldn' be satisfied ef he gin Sandy ter a'er one un 'em; so w'en dey wuz all done married, he fix it by 'lowin' one er his chilluns ter take Sandy fer a mont' er so, en den ernudder for a mont' er so, en so on dat erway tel dey had all had 'im de same lenk er time; en den dey would all take him roun' ag'in, 'cep'n oncet in a w'ile w'en Mars Marrabo would len' 'im ter some er his yuther kinfolks 'roun' de country, w'en dey wuz short er han's; tel bimeby it got so Sandy didn' hardly knowed whar he wuz gwine ter stay fum one week's een' ter de yuther.

"One time w'en Sandy wuz lent out ez yushal, a spekilater come erlong wid a lot er niggers, en Mars Marrabo swap' Sandy's wife off fer a noo 'oman. W'en Sandy come back, Mars Marrabo gin 'im a dollar, en 'lowed he wuz monst'us sorry fer ter break up de fambly, but de spekilater had gin 'im big boot, en times wuz hard en money skase, en so he wuz bleedst ter make de trade. Sandy tuk on some 'bout losin' his wife, but he soon seed dey want no use cryin' ober spilt merlasses; en bein' ez he lacked de looks er de noo 'oman, he tuk up wid her atter she'd be'n on de plantation a mont' er so.

"Sandy en his noo wife got on mighty well tergedder, en de niggers all 'mence' ter talk about how lovin' dey wuz. W'en Tenie wuz tuk sick oncet, Sandy useter set up all night wid 'er, en den go ter wuk in de mawnin' des lack he had his reg'lar sleep; en Tenie would 'a' done anythin' in de worl' for her Sandy.

"Sandy en Tenie hadn' be'n libbin' tergedder fer mo' d'n two mont's befo' Mars Marrabo's old uncle, w'at libbed down in Robeson County, sent up ter fin' out ef Mars Marrabo couldn' len' 'im er hire 'im a good han' fer a mont' er so. Sandy's marster wuz one er dese yer easy-gwine folks w'at wanter please eve'ybody, en he says yas, he could len' 'im Sandy. En Mars Marrabo tol' Sandy fer ter git ready ter go down ter Robeson nex' day, fer ter stay a mont' er so.

"It wuz monst'us hard on Sandy fer ter take 'im 'way fum Tenie. It wuz so fur down ter Robeson dat he didn' hab no chance er comin' back ter see her tel de time wuz up; he wouldn' 'a' mine comin' ten er fifteen mile at night ter see Tenie, but Mars Marrabo's uncle's plantation wuz mo' d'n forty mile off. Sandy wuz mighty sad en cas' down atter w'at Mars Marrabo tol' 'im, en he says ter Tenie, sezee:—

"'I'm gittin' monst'us ti'ed er dish yer gwine roun' so much. Here I is lent ter Mars Jeems dis mont', en I got ter do so-en-so; en ter Mars Archie de nex' mont', en I got ter do so-en-so; den I got ter go ter Miss Jinnie's: en hit's Sandy dis en Sandy dat, en Sandy yer en Sandy dere, tel it 'pears ter me I ain' got no home, ner no marster, ner no mistiss, ner no nuffin. I can't eben keep a wife: my yuther ole 'oman wuz sol' away widout my gittin' a chance fer ter tell her good-by; en now I got ter go off en leab you, Tenie, en I dunno whe'r I'm eber gwine ter see you ag'in er no. I wisht I wuz a tree, er a stump, er a rock, er sump'n w'at could stay on de plantation fer a w'ile.'

"Atter Sandy got thoo talkin', Tenie didn' say naer word, but des sot dere by de fier, studyin' en studyin'. Bimeby she up'n' says:—

"'Sandy, is I eber tol' you I wuz a cunjuh 'oman?'

"Co'se Sandy hadn' nebber dremp' er nuffin lack dat, en he made a great 'miration w'en he hear w'at Tenie say. Bimeby Tenie went on:—

"'I ain' goophered nobody, ner done no cunjuh wuk, fer fifteen year er mo'; en w'en I got religion I made up my mine I wouldn' wuk no mo' goopher. But dey is some things I doan b'lieve it's no sin fer'ter do; en ef you doan wanter be sent roun' fum pillar ter pos', en ef you doan wanter go down ter Robeson, I kin fix things so you won't haf ter. Ef you'll des say de word, I kin turn you ter w'ateber you wanter be, en you kin stay right whar you wanter, ez long ez you mineter.'

"Sandy say he doan keer; he's willin' fer ter do anythin' fer ter stay close ter Tenie. Den Tenie ax 'im ef he doan wanter be turnt inter a rabbit.

"Sandy say, 'No, de dogs mought git atter me.'

"'Shill I turn you ter a wolf?' sez Tenie.

"'No, eve'ybody's skeered er a wolf, en I doan want nobody ter be skeered er me.'

"'Shill I turn you ter a mawkin'-bird?'

"'No, a hawk mought ketch me. I wanter be turnt inter sump'n w'at'll stay in one place.'

"'I kin turn you ter a tree,' sez Tenie. 'You won't hab no mouf ner years, but I kin turn you back oncet in a w'ile, so you kin git sump'n ter eat, en hear w'at's gwine on.'

"Well, Sandy say dat'll do. En so Tenie tuk 'im down by de aidge er de swamp, not fur fum de quarters, en turnt 'im inter a big pine-tree, en sot 'im out 'mongs' some yuther trees. En de nex' mawnin', ez some er de fiel' han's wuz gwine long dere, dey seed a tree w'at dey didn' 'member er habbin' seed befo'; it wuz monst'us quare, en dey wuz bleedst ter 'low dat dey hadn' 'membered right, er e'se one er de saplin's had be'n growin' monst'us fas'.

"W'en Mars Marrabo 'skiver' dat Sandy wuz gone, he 'lowed Sandy had runned away. He got de dogs out, but de las' place dey could track Sandy ter wuz de foot er dat pine-tree. En dere de dogs stood en barked, en bayed, en pawed at de tree, en tried ter climb up on it; en w'en dey wuz tuk roun' thoo de swamp ter look fer de scent, dey broke loose en made fer dat tree ag'in. It wuz de beatenis' thing de w'ite folks eber hearn of, en Mars Marrabo 'lowed dat Sandy must 'a' clim' up on de tree en jump' off on a mule er sump'n, en rid fur ernuff fer ter spile de scent. Mars Marrabo wanted ter 'cuse some er de yuther niggers er heppin' Sandy off, but dey all 'nied it ter de las'; en eve'ybody knowed Tenie sot too much sto' by Sandy fer ter he'p 'im run away whar she couldn' nebber see 'im no mo'.

"W'en Sandy had be'n gone long ernuff fer folks ter think he done got clean away, Tenie useter go down ter de woods at night en turn 'im back, en den dey'd slip up ter de cabin en set by de fire en talk. But dey ha' ter be monst'us keerful, er e'se somebody would 'a' seed 'em, en dat would 'a' spile' de whole thing; so Tenie alluz turnt Sandy back in de mawnin' early, befo' anybody wuz a-stirrin'.

"But Sandy didn't git erlong widout his trials en tribberlations. One day a woodpecker come erlong en 'mence' ter peck at de tree; en de nex' time Sandy wuz turnt back he had a little roun' hole in his arm, des lack a sharp stick be'n stuck in it. Atter dat Tenie sot a sparrer-hawk fer ter watch de tree; en w'en de woodpecker come erlong nex' mawnin' fer ter finish his nes', he got gobble' up mos' 'fo' he stuck his bill in de bark.

"Nudder time, Mars Marrabo sent a nigger out in de woods fer ter chop tuppentime boxes. De man chop a box in dish yer tree, en hack' de bark up two er th'ee feet, fer ter let de tuppentime run. De nex' time Sandy wuz turnt back he had a big skyar on his lef' leg, des lack it be'n skunt; en it tuk Tenie nigh 'bout all night fer ter fix a mixtry ter kyo it up. Atter dat, Tenie sot a hawnet fer ter watch de tree; en w'en de nigger come back ag'in fer ter cut ernudder box on de yuther side 'n de tree, de hawnet stung 'im so hard dat de ax slip en cut his foot nigh 'bout off.

"W'en Tenie see so many things happenin' ter de tree, she 'cluded she'd ha' ter turn Sandy ter sump'n e'se; en atter studyin' de matter ober, en talkin' wid Sandy one ebenin', she made up her mine fer ter fix up a goopher mixtry w'at would turn herse'f en Sandy ter foxes, er sump'n, so dey could run away en go some'rs whar dey could be free en lib lack w'ite folks.

"But dey ain' no tellin' w'at's gwine ter happen in dis worl'. Tenie had got de night sot fer her en Sandy ter run away, w'en dat ve'y day one er Mars Marrabo's sons rid up ter de big house in his buggy, en say his wife wuz monst'us sick, en he want his mammy ter len' 'im a 'oman fer ter nuss his wife. Tenie's mistiss say sen' Tenie; she wuz a good nuss. Young mars wuz in a tarrible hurry fer ter git back home. Tenie wuz washin' at de big house dat day, en her mistiss say she should go right 'long wid her young marster. Tenie tried ter make some 'scuse fer ter git away en hide 'tel night, w'en she would have eve'ything fix' up fer her en Sandy; she say she wanter go ter her cabin fer ter git her bonnet. Her mistiss say it doan matter 'bout de bonnet; her head-hankcher wuz good ernuff. Den Tenie say she wanter git her bes' frock; her mistiss say

no, she doan need no mo' frock, en w'en dat one got dirty she could git
a clean one whar she wuz gwine. So Tenie had ter git in de buggy en
go 'long wid young Mars Dunkin ter his plantation, w'ich wuz mo' d'n
twenty mile away; en dey wa'n't no chance er her seein' Sandy no mo'
'tel she come back home. De po' gal felt monst'us bad 'bout de way
things wuz gwine on, en she knowed Sandy mus' be a wond'rin' why
she didn' come en turn 'im back no mo'.

"W'iles Tenie wuz away nussin' young Mars Dunkin's wife, Mars
Marrabo tuk a notion fer ter buil' 'im a noo kitchen; en bein' ez he had
lots er timber on his place, he begun ter look 'roun' fer a tree ter hab
de lumber sawed out'n. En I dunno how it come to be so, but he happen fer ter hit on de ve'y tree w'at Sandy wuz turnt inter. Tenie wuz
gone, en dey wa'n't nobody ner nuffin fer ter watch de tree.

"De two men w'at cut de tree down say dey nebber had sech a time
wid a tree befo': dey axes would glansh off, en didn' 'pear ter make no
progress thoo de wood; en of all de creakin', en shakin', en wobblin'
you eber see, dat tree done it w'en it commence' ter fall. It wuz de beatenis' thing!

"W'en dey got de tree all trim' up, dey chain it up ter a timber waggin, en start fer de sawmill. But dey had a hard time gittin' de log dere:
fus' dey got stuck in de mud w'en dey wuz gwine crosst de swamp, en
it wuz two er th'ee hours befo' dey could git out. W'en dey start' on
ag'in, de chain kep' a-comin' loose, en dey had ter keep a-stoppin' en
a-stoppin' fer ter hitch de log up ag'in. W'en dey commence' ter climb
de hill ter de sawmill, de log broke loose, en roll down de hill en in
'mongs' de trees, en hit tuk nigh 'bout half a day mo' ter git it haul' up
ter de sawmill.

"De nex' mawnin' atter de day de tree wuz haul' ter de sawmill,
Tenie come home. W'en she got back ter her cabin, de fus' thing she
done wuz ter run down ter de woods en see how Sandy wuz gittin' on.
W'en she seed de stump standin' dere, wid de sap runnin' out'n it, en
de limbs layin' scattered roun', she nigh 'bout went out'n her min'. She
run ter her cabin, en got her goopher mixtry, en den follered de track
er de timber waggin ter de sawmill. She knowed Sandy couldn' lib mo'
d'n a minute er so ef she turnt him back, fer he wuz all chop' up so he'd
'a' be'n bleedst ter die. But she wanted ter turn 'im back long ernuff fer
ter 'splain ter 'im dat she hadn't went off a-purpose, en lef' 'im ter be
chop' down en sawed up. She didn' want Sandy ter die wid no hard
feelin's to'ds her.

"De han's at de sawmill had des got de big log on de kerridge, en wuz
startin' up de saw, w'en dey seed a 'oman runnin' up de hill, all out er
bref, cryin' en gwine on des lack she wuz plumb 'stracted. It wuz Tenie;
she come right inter de mill, en th'owed herse'f on de log, right in front

er de saw, a-hollerin' en cryin' ter her Sandy ter fergib her, en not ter
think hard er her, fer it wa'n't no fault er hern. Den Tenie 'membered
de tree didn' hab no years, en she wuz gittin' ready fer ter wuk her goopher mixtry so ez ter turn Sandy back, w'en de mill-hands kotch holt er
her en tied her arms wid a rope, en fasten' her to one er de posts in de
sawmill; en den dey started de saw up ag'in, en cut de log up inter bo'ds
en scantlin's right befo' her eyes. But it wuz mighty hard wuk; fer of all
de sweekin', en moanin', en groanin', dat log done it w'iles de saw wuz
a-cuttin' thoo it. De saw wuz one er dese yer ole-timey, up-en-down
saws, en hit tuk longer dem days ter saw a log 'en it do now. Dey greased
de saw, but dat didn' stop de fuss; hit kep' right on, tel fin'ly dey got de
log all sawed up.

"W'en de oberseah w'at run de sawmill come fum breakfas', de han's
up en tell him 'bout de crazy 'oman—ez dey s'posed she wuz—w'at
had come runnin' in de sawmill, a-hollerin' en gwine on, en tried ter
th'ow herse'f befo' de saw. En de oberseah sent two er th'ee er de han's
fer ter take Tenie back ter her marster's plantation.

"Tenie 'peared ter be out'n her min' fer a long time, en her marster
ha' ter lock her up in de smoke-'ouse 'tel she got ober her spells. Mars
Marrabo wuz monst'us mad, en hit would 'a' made yo' flesh crawl fer
ter hear him cuss, 'caze he say de spekilater w'at he got Tenie fum had
fooled 'im by wukkin' a crazy 'oman off on him. W'iles Tenie wuz lock
up in de smoke-'ouse, Mars Marrabo tuk 'n' haul de lumber fum de
sawmill, en put up his noo kitchen.

"W'en Tenie got quiet' down, so she could be 'lowed ter go 'roun' de
plantation, she up 'n' tole her marster all erbout Sandy en de pine-tree;
en w'en Mars Marrabo hearn it, he 'lowed she wuz de wuss 'stracted
nigger he eber hearn of. He didn' know w'at ter do wid Tenie: fus' he
thought he'd put her in de po'-house; but fin'ly, seein' ez she didn' do
no harm ter nobody ner nuffin, but des went 'roun' moanin', en
groanin', en shakin' her head, he 'cluded ter let her stay on de plantation en nuss de little nigger chilluns w'en dey mammies wuz ter wuk
in de cotton-fiel'.

"De noo kitchen Mars Marrabo buil' wuzn' much use, fer it hadn'
be'n put up long befo' de niggers 'mence' ter notice quare things erbout it. Dey could hear sump'n moanin' en groanin' 'bout de kitchen
in de night-time, en w'en de win' would blow dey could hear sump'n
a-hollerin' en sweekin' lack it wuz in great pain en sufferin'. En it got
so atter a w'ile dat it wuz all Mars Marrabo's wife could do ter git a
'oman ter stay in de kitchen in de daytime long ernuff ter do de
cookin'; en dey wa'n't naer nigger on de plantation w'at wouldn' rud-
der take forty dan ter go 'bout dat kitchen atter dark,—dat is, 'cep'n'

Tenie; she didn' 'pear ter min' de ha'nts. She useter slip 'roun' at night, en set on de kitchen steps, en lean up agin de do'-jamb, en run on ter herse'f wid some kine er foolishness w'at nobody couldn' make out; fer Mars Marrabo had th'eaten' ter sen' her off'n de plantation ef she say anything ter any er de yuther niggers 'bout de pine-tree. But somehow er 'nudder de niggers foun' out all erbout it, en dey all knowed de kitchen wuz ha'nted by Sandy's sperrit. En bimeby hit got so Mars Marrabo's wife herse'f wuz skeered ter go out in de yard atter dark.

"W'en it come ter dat, Mars Marrabo tuk en to' de kitchen down, en use' de lumber fer ter buil' dat ole school'ouse w'at you er talkin' 'bout pullin' down. De school'ouse wuzn' use' 'cep'n' in de daytime, en on dark nights folks gwine 'long de road would hear quare soun's en see quare things. Po' ole Tenie useter go down dere at night, en wander 'roun' de school'ouse; en de niggers all 'lowed she went fer ter talk wid Sandy's sperrit. En one winter mawnin', w'en one er de boys went ter school early fer ter start de fire, w'at should he fin' but po' ole Tenie, layin' on de flo', stiff, en col', en dead. Dere didn' 'pear ter be nuffin pertickler de matter wid her,—she had des grieve' herse'f ter def fer her Sandy. Mars Marrabo didn' shed no tears. He thought Tenie wuz crazy, en dey wa'n't no tellin' w'at she mought do nex'; en dey ain' much room in dis worl' fer crazy w'ite folks, let 'lone a crazy nigger.

"Hit wa'n't long atter dat befo' Mars Marrabo sol' a piece er his track er lan' ter Mars Dugal' McAdoo,—my ole marster,—en dat's how de ole school'ouse happen to be on yo' place. W'en de wah broke out, de school stop', en de ole school'ouse be'n stannin' empty ever sence,— dat is, 'cep'n' fer de ha'nts. En folks sez dat de ole school'ouse, er any yuther house w'at got any er dat lumber in it w'at wuz sawed out'n de tree w'at Sandy wuz turnt inter, is gwine ter be ha'nted tel de las' piece er plank is rotted en crumble' inter dus'.'"

Annie had listened to this gruesome narrative with strained attention. "What a system it was," she exclaimed, when Julius had finished, "under which such things were possible!"

"What things?" I asked, in amazement. "Are you seriously considering the possibility of a man's being turned into a tree?"

"Oh, no," she replied quickly, "not that"; and then she murmured absently, and with a dim look in her fine eyes, "Poor Tenie!"

We ordered the lumber, and returned home. That night, after we had gone to bed, and my wife had to all appearances been sound asleep for half an hour, she startled me out of an incipient doze by exclaiming suddenly,—

"John, I don't believe I want my new kitchen built out of the lumber in that old schoolhouse."

"You wouldn't for a moment allow yourself," I replied, with some asperity, "to be influenced by that absurdly impossible yarn which Julius was spinning to-day?"

"I know the story is absurd," she replied dreamily, "and I am not so silly as to believe it. But I don't think I should ever be able to take any pleasure in that kitchen if it were built out of that lumber. Besides, I think the kitchen would look better and last longer if the lumber were all new."

Of course she had her way. I bought the new lumber, though not without grumbling. A week or two later I was called away from home on business. On my return, after an absence of several days, my wife remarked to me,—

"John, there has been a split in the Sandy Run Colored Baptist Church, on the temperance question. About half the members have come out from the main body, and set up for themselves. Uncle Julius is one of the seceders, and he came to me yesterday and asked if they might not hold their meetings in the old schoolhouse for the present."

"I hope you didn't let the old rascal have it," I returned, with some warmth. I had just received a bill for the new lumber I had bought.

"Well," she replied, "I couldn't refuse him the use of the house for so good a purpose."

"And I'll venture to say," I continued, "that you subscribed something toward the support of the new church?"

She did not attempt to deny it.

"What are they going to do about the ghost?" I asked, somewhat curious to know how Julius would get around this obstacle.

"Oh," replied Annie, "Uncle Julius says that ghosts never disturb religious worship, but that if Sandy's spirit *should* happen to stray into meeting by mistake, no doubt the preaching would do it good."

DAVE'S NECKLISS

"HAVE SOME dinner, Uncle Julius?" said my wife.

It was a Sunday afternoon in early autumn. Our two women-servants had gone to a camp-meeting some miles away, and would not return until evening. My wife had served the dinner, and we were just rising from the table, when Julius came up the lane, and, taking off his hat, seated himself on the piazza.

The old man glanced through the open door at the dinner table, and his eyes rested lovingly upon a large sugar-cured ham, from which several slices had been cut, exposing a rich pink expanse that would have appealed strongly to the appetite of any hungry Christian.

"Thanky, Miss Annie," he said, after a momentary hesitation, "I dunno ez I keers ef I does tas'e a piece er dat ham—ef yer'll cut me off a slice un it."

"No," said Annie, "I won't. Just sit down to the table and help yourself; eat all you want, and don't be bashful."

Julius drew a chair up to the table, while my wife and I went out on the piazza. Julius was in my employment; he took his meals with his own family, but when he happened to be about our house at meal times, my wife never let him go away hungry.

I threw myself into a hammock, from which I could see Julius through an open window. He ate with evident relish, devoting his attention chiefly to the ham, slice after slice of which disappeared in the spacious cavity of his mouth. At first the old man ate rapidly, but after the edge of his appetite had been taken off he proceeded in a more leisurely manner. When he had cut the sixth slice of ham (I kept count of them from a lazy curiosity to see how much he *could* eat) I saw him lay it on his plate; as he adjusted the knife and fork to cut it into smaller pieces, he paused, as if struck by a sudden thought, and a tear rolled down his rugged cheek and fell upon the slice of ham before him. But the emotion, whatever the thought that caused it, was

21

transitory, and in a moment he continued his dinner. When he was through eating, he came out on the porch, and resumed his seat with the satisfied expression of countenance that usually follows a good dinner.

"Julius," I said, "you seemed to be affected by something, a moment ago. Was the mustard so strong that it moved you to tears?"

"No, suh, it wa'n't de mustard; I wuz studyin' 'bout Dave."

"Who was Dave, and what about him?" I asked.

The conditions were all favorable to story-telling. There was an autumnal languor in the air, and a dreamy haze softened the dark green of the distant pines and the deep blue of the Southern sky. The generous meal he had made had put the old man in a very good humor. He was not always so, for his curiously undeveloped nature was subject to moods which were almost childish in their variableness. It was only now and then that we were able to study, through the medium of his recollection, the simple but intensely human inner life of slavery. His way of looking at the past seemed very strange to us; his view of certain sides of life was essentially different from ours. He never indulged in any regrets for the Arcadian joyousness and irresponsibility which was a somewhat popular conception of slavery; his had not been the lot of the petted house-servant, but that of the toiling field-hand. While he mentioned with a warm appreciation the acts of kindness which those in authority had shown to him and his people, he would speak of a cruel deed, not with the indignation of one accustomed to quick feeling and spontaneous expression, but with a furtive disapproval which suggested to us a doubt in his own mind as to whether he had a right to think or to feel, and presented to us the curious psychological spectacle of a mind enslaved long after the shackles had been struck off from the limbs of its possessor. Whether the sacred name of liberty ever set his soul aglow with a generous fire; whether he had more than the most elementary ideas of love, friendship, patriotism, religion—things which are half, and the better half, of life to us; whether he even realized, except in a vague, uncertain way, his own degradation, I do not know. I fear not; and if not, then centuries of repression had borne their legitimate fruit. But in the simple human feeling, and still more in the undertone of sadness, which pervaded his stories, I thought I could see a spark which, fanned by favoring breezes and fed by the memories of the past, might become in his children's children a glowing flame of sensibility, alive to every thrill of human happiness or human woe.

"Dave use' ter b'long ter my ole marster," said Julius; "he wuz raise' on dis yer plantation, en I kin 'member all erbout 'im, fer I wuz ole 'nuff ter chop cotton w'en it all happen'. Dave wuz a tall man, en monst'us strong: he could do mo' wuk in a day dan any yuther two niggers on de plantation. He wuz one er dese yer solemn kine er men, en nebber run on wid much foolishness, like de yuther darkies. He use' ter go out in de woods en pray; en w'en he hear de han's on de plantation cussin' en gwine on wid dere dancin' en foolishness, he use' ter tell 'em 'bout religion en jedgemen'-day, w'en dey would haf ter gin account for eve'y idle word en all dey yuther sinful kyarin's on.

"Dave had l'arn how ter read de Bible. Dey wuz a free nigger boy in de settlement w'at wuz monst'us smart, en could write en cipher, en wuz alluz readin' books er papers. En Dave had hi'ed dis free boy fer to l'arn 'im how ter read. Hit wuz 'g'in' de law, but co'se none er de niggers didn' say nuffin ter de w'ite folks 'bout it. Howsomedever, one day Mars Walker—he wuz de oberseah—foun' out Dave could read. Mars Walker wa'n't nuffin but a po' bockrah, en folks said he couldn' read ner write hisse'f, en co'se he didn' lack ter see a nigger w'at knowed mo' d'n he did; so he went en tole Mars Dugal'. Mars Dugal' sont fer Dave, en ax' 'im 'bout it.

"Dave didn't hardly knowed w'at ter do; but he couldn' tell no lie, so he 'fessed he could read de Bible a little by spellin' out de words. Mars Dugal' look' mighty solemn.

"'Dis yer is a se'ious matter,' sezee; 'it's 'g'in de law ter l'arn niggers how ter read, er 'low 'em ter hab books. But w'at yer l'arn out'n dat Bible, Dave?'

"Dave wa'n't no fool, ef he wuz a nigger, en sezee:

"'Marster, I l'arns dat it's a sin fer ter steal, er ter lie, er fer ter want w'at doan b'long ter yer; en I l'arns fer ter love de Lawd en ter 'bey my marster.'

"Mars Dugal' sorter smile' en laf' ter hisse'f, like he 'uz might'ly tickle' 'bout sump'n, en sezee:

"'Doan 'pear ter me lack readin' de Bible done yer much harm, Dave. Dat's w'at I wants all my niggers fer ter know. Yer keep right on readin', en tell de yuther han's w'at yer be'n tellin' me. How would yer lack fer ter preach ter de niggers on Sunday?'

"Dave say he'd be glad fer ter do w'at he could. So Mars Dugal' tole de oberseah fer ter let Dave preach ter de niggers, en tell 'em w'at wuz in de Bible, en it would he'p ter keep 'em fum stealin' er runnin' erway.

"So Dave 'mence' ter preach, en done de han's on de plantation a heap er good, en most un 'em lef' off dey wicked ways, en 'mence' ter love ter hear 'bout God, en religion, en de Bible; en dey done dey wuk better, en didn' gib de oberseah but mighty little trouble fer to manage 'em.

"Dave wuz one er dese yer men w'at didn' keer much fer de gals—leastways he didn' 'tel Dilsey come ter de plantation. Dilsey wuz a monst'us peart, good-lookin', gingybread-colored gal—one er dese high-steppin' gals w'at hol's dey head up, en won' stan' no foolishness fum no man. She had b'long ter a gemman over on Rockfish w'at died, en whose 'state ha' ter be sol' fer ter pay his debts. En Mars Dugal' had be'n ter de oction, en w'en he seed dis gal a-cryin' en gwine on 'bout bein' sol' erway fum her ole mammy, Aun' Mahaly, Mars Dugal' bid 'em bofe in, en fotch 'em ober ter our plantation.

"De young nigger men on de plantation wuz des wil' atter Dilsey, but it didn' do no good, en none un 'em couldn' git Dilsey fer dey junesey, 'tel Dave 'mence' fer ter go roun' Aun' Mahaly's cabin. Dey wuz a fine-lookin' couple, Dave en Dilsey wuz, bofe tall, en well-shape', en soopl'. En dey sot a heap by one ernudder. Mars Dugal' seed 'em tergedder one Sunday, en de nex' time he seed Dave atter dat, sezee:

"'Dave, w'en yer en Dilsey gits ready fer ter git married, I ain' got no rejections. Dey's a poun' er so er chawin'-terbacker up at de house, en I reckon yo' mist'iss kin fine a frock en a ribbin er two fer Dilsey. You er bofe good niggers, en yer neenter be feared er ein' sol' 'way fum one ernudder long ez I owns dis plantation; en I 'spec' ter own it fer a long time yit.'

"But dere wuz one man on de plantation w'at didn' lack ter see Dave en Dilsey tergedder ez much ez marster did. W'en Mars Dugal' went ter de sale whar he got Dilsey en Mahaly, he bought ernudder han', by de name er Wiley. Wiley wuz one er dese yer shiny-eyed, double-headed little niggers, sha'p ez a steel trap, en sly ez de fox w'at keep out'n it. Dis yer Wiley had be'n pesterin' Dilsey 'fo' she come ter our plantation, en had nigh 'bout worried de life out'n her. She didn' keer nuffin fer 'im, but he pestered her so she ha' ter th'eaten ter tell her marster fer ter make Wiley let her 'lone. W'en he come ober to our place it wuz des ez bad, 'tel bimeby Wiley seed dat Dilsey had got ter thinkin' a heap 'bout Dave, en den he sorter hilt off aw'ile, en purten' lack he gin Dilsey up. But he wuz one er dese yer 'ceitful niggers, en w'ile he wuz laffin' en jokin' wid de yuther han's 'bout Dave en Dilsey, he wuz settin' a trap fer ter ketch Dave en git Dilsey back fer hisse'f.

"Dave en Dilsey made up dere min's fer ter git married long 'bout Christmas time, w'en dey'd hab mo' time fer a weddin'. But 'long 'bout two weeks befo' dat time ole Mars 'mence' ter lose a heap er bacon. Eve'y night er so somebody 'ud steal a side er bacon, er a ham, er a shoulder, er sump'n fum one er de smoke-'ouses. De smoke-'ouses wuz lock', but somebody had a key, en manage' ter git in some way er 'nudder. Dey's mo' ways 'n one ter skin a cat, en dey's mo' d'n one way ter git in a smoke-'ouse—leastways dat's w'at I hearn say. Folks w'at had bacon fer ter sell didn' hab no trouble 'bout gittin' rid un it. Hit wuz 'g'in de law fer ter buy things fum slabes; but Lawd! dat law didn' 'mount ter a hill er peas. Eve'y week er so one er dese yer big covered waggins would come 'long de road, peddlin' terbacker en w'iskey. Dey

wuz a sight er room in one er dem big waggins, en it wuz monst'us easy
fer ter swop off bacon fer sump'n ter chaw er ter wa'm yer up in de
winter-time. I s'pose de peddlers didn' knowed dey wuz breakin' de law,
caze de niggers alluz went at night, en stayed on de dark side er de
waggin; en it wuz mighty yard fer ter tell *w'at* kine er folks dey wuz.

"Atter two er th'ee hund'ed pounds er meat had be'n stol', Mars
Walker call all de niggers up one eben', en tol' 'em dat de fus' nigger he
cot stealin' bacon on dat plantation would git sump'n fer ter 'member it
by long ez he lib'. En he say he'd gin fi' dollars ter de nigger w'at 'skiver'
de rogue. Mars Walker say he s'picion one er two er de niggers, but he
couldn' tell fer sho, en co'se dey all 'nied it w'en he 'cuse 'em un it.

"Dey wa'n't no bacon stole' fer a week er so, 'tel one dark night w'en
somebody tuk a ham fum one er de smoke-'ouses. Mars Walker des
cusst awful w'en he foun' out de ham wuz gone, en say he gwine ter
sarch all de niggers' cabins; w'en dis yer Wiley I wuz tellin' yer 'bout
up'n say he s'picion' who tuk de ham, fer he seed Dave comin' 'cross
de plantation fum to'ds de smoke-'ouse de night befo'. W'en Mars
Walker hearn dis fum Wiley, he went en sarch' Dave's cabin, en foun'
de ham hid under de flo'.

"Eve'ybody wuz 'stonish'; but dere wuz de ham. Co'se Dave 'nied it
ter de las', but dere wuz de ham. Mars Walker say it wuz des ez he
'spected: he didn' b'lieve in dese yer readin' en prayin' niggers; it wuz
all 'pocrisy, en sarve' Mars Dugal' right fer 'lowin' Dave ter be readin'
books w'en it wuz 'g'in' de law.

"W'en Mars Dugal' hearn 'bout de ham, he say he wuz might'ly
'ceived en disapp'inted in Dave. He say he wouldn' nebber hab no mo'
conference in no nigger, en Mars Walker could do des ez he wuz a
mineter wid Dave er any er de res' er de niggers. So Mars Walker tuk'n
tied Dave up en gin 'im forty; en den he got some er dis yer wire clof
w'at dey uses fer to make sifters out'n en tuk'n wrap' it roun' de ham en
fasten it tergedder at de little een'. Den he tuk Dave down ter de
blacksmif shop, en had Unker Silas, de plantation blacksmif, fasten a
chain ter de ham, en den fasten de yuther een' er de chain roun' Dave's
neck. En den he says ter Dave, sezee:

"'Now, suh, yer'll wear dat neckliss fer de nex' six mont's; en I 'spec's
yer ner none er de yuther niggers on dis plantation won' steal no mo'
bacon dyoin' er dat time.'

"Well, it des 'peared ez if fum dat time Dave didn' hab nuffin but
trouble. De niggers all turnt ag'in 'im, caze he be'n de 'casion er Mars
Dugal' turnin' 'em all ober ter Mars Walker. Mars Dugal' wa'n't a bad
marster hisse'f, but Mars Walker wuz hard ez a rock. Dave kep' on
sayin' he didn' take de ham, but none un 'em didn' b'lieve him.

"Dilsey wa'n't on de plantation w'en Dave wuz 'cused er stealin' de bacon. Ole Mist'iss had sont her ter town fer a week er so fer ter wait on one er her darters w'at had a young baby, en she didn' fine out nuffin' 'bout Dave's trouble 'tel she got back ter de plantation. Dave had patien'ly endyoed de finger er scawn, en all de hard words w'at de niggers pile' on 'im, caze he wuz sho' Dilsey would stan' by 'im, en wouldn' b'lieve he wuz a rogue, ner none er de yuther tales de darkies wuz tellin' 'bout 'im.

"W'en Dilsey come back fum town, en got down fum behine de buggy whar she b'en ridin' wid ole Mars, de fus' nigger 'oman she met says ter her,

"'Is yer seed Dave, Dilsey?'

"'No, I ain' seed Dave,' says Dilsey.

"'Yer des oughter look at dat nigger; reckon yer wouldn' want 'im fer yo' junesey no mo'. Mars Walker cotch 'im stealin' bacon, en gone en fasten' a ham roun' his neck, so he can't git it off'n hisse'f. He sut'nly do look quare.' En den de 'oman bus' out laffin' fit ter kill herse'f. W'en she got thoo laffin' she up'n tole Dilsey all 'bout de ham, en all de yuther lies w'at de niggers be'n tellin' on Dave.

"W'en Dilsey started down ter de quarters, who should she meet but Dave, comin' in fum de cotton-fiel'. She turnt her head ter one side, en purten' lack she didn' seed Dave.

"'Dilsey!' sezee.

"Dilsey walk' right on, en didn' notice 'im.

"'*Oh*, Dilsey!'

"Dilsey didn' paid no 'tention ter 'im, en den Dave knowed some er de niggers be'n tellin' her 'bout de ham. He felt monst'us bad, but he 'lowed ef he could des git Dilsey fer ter listen ter 'im fer a minute er so, he could make her b'lieve he didn' stole de bacon. It wuz a week er two befo' he could git a chance ter speak ter her ag'in; but fine'ly he cotch her down by de spring one day, en sezee:

"'Dilsey, w'at fer yer won' speak ter me, en purten' lack yer doan see me? Dilsey, yer knows me too well fer ter b'lieve I'd steal, er do dis yuther wick'ness de niggers is all layin' ter me—yer *knows* I wouldn' do dat, Dilsey. Yer ain' gwine back on yo' Dave, is yer?'

"But w'at Dave say didn' hab no 'fec' on Dilsey. Dem lies folks b'en tellin' her had p'isen her min' 'g'n Dave.

"'I doan wanter talk ter no nigger,' says she, 'w'at be'n whip' fer stealin', en w'at gwine roun' wid such a lookin' thing ez dat hung roun' his neck. I's a 'spectable gal, *I* is. W'at yer call dat, Dave? Is dat a cha'm fer ter keep off witches, er is it a noo kine er neckliss yer got?'

"Po' Dave didn' knowed w'at ter do. De las' one he had 'pended on fer ter stan' by 'im had gone back on 'im, en dey didn' 'pear ter be nuffin mo' wuf libbin' fer. He couldn' hol' no mo' pra'r-meetin's, fer Mars

Walker wouldn' 'low 'im ter preach, en de darkies wouldn' a' listen' ter
'im ef he had preach'. He didn' eben hab his Bible fer ter comfort
hisse'f wid, fer Mars Walker had tuk it erway fum 'im en burnt it up, en
say ef he kotch any mo' niggers wid Bibles on de plantation, he'd do
'em wuss'n he done Dave.

"En ter make it still harder fer Dave, Dilsey tuk up wid Wiley. Dave
could see him gwine up ter Aun' Mahaly's cabin, en settin' out on de
bench in de moonlight wid Dilsey, en singin' sinful songs en playin' de
banjer. Dave use' ter scrouch down behine de bushes, en wonder w'at
de Lawd sen' 'im all dem tribberlations fer.

"But all er Dave's yuther troubles w'a'n't nuffin side er dat ham. He
had wrap' de chain roun' wid a rag, so it didn' hurt his neck; but
w'eneber he went ter wuk, dat ham would be in his way; he had ter do
his task, howsomedever, des de same ez ef he didn' hab de ham.
W'eneber he went ter lay down, dat ham would be in de way. Ef he
turn ober in his sleep, dat ham would be tuggin' at his neck. It wuz de
las' thing he seed at night, en de fus' thing he seed in de mawnin'.
W'eneber he met a stranger, de ham would be de fus' thing de stranger
would see. Most un 'em would 'mence' ter laf, en whareber Dave went
he could see folks p'intin' at him, en year 'em sayin':

"'W'at kine er collar dat nigger got roun' his neck?' er, ef dey knowed
'im, 'Is yer stole any mo' hams lately?' er 'W'at yer take fer yo' neckliss,
Dave?'

"Fus' Dave didn' mine it so much, caze he knowed he hadn' done
nuffin. But bimeby he got so he couldn' stan it no longer, en he'd hide
hisse'f in de bushes w'eneber he seed anybody comin', en alluz kep'
hisse'f shet up in his cabin atter he come in fum wuk.

"It wuz monst'us hard on Dave, en bimeby, w'at wid dat ham eber-
lastin' en eternally draggin' roun' his neck, he 'mence' fer ter do en say
quare things, en make de niggers wonder ef he wa'n't gittin' out'n his
mine. He got ter gwine roun' talkin' ter hisse'f, en singin' corn-shuckin'
songs, en laffin' fit ter kill 'bout nuffin. En one day he tole one er de
niggers he had 'skivered a noo way fer ter raise hams—gwine ter pick
'em off'm trees, en save de expense er smoke-'ouses by kyoin' 'em in de
sun. En one day he up'n tole Mars Walker he got sump'n pertickler fer
ter say ter 'im; en tole 'im he wuz gwine ter show 'im a place in de
swamp whar dey wuz a whole trac' er lan' covered wid ham-trees.

"W'en Mars Walker hearn Dave talkin' dis kine er fool-talk, en w'en
he seed how Dave wuz 'mencin' ter git behine in his wuk, en w'en he
ax' de niggers en dey tole 'im how Dave be'n gwine on, he 'lowed he
reckon' he'd punish' Dave ernuff, en it mou't do mo' harm dan good
fer ter keep de ham on his neck any longer. So he sont Dave down ter
de blacksmifshop en had de ham tuk off. Dey wa'n't much er de ham

lef' by dat time, fer de sun had melt all de fat, en de lean had all swivel' up, so dey wa'n't but th'ee er fo' poun's lef'.

"W'en de ham had be'n tuk off'n Dave, folks kinder stopped talkin' 'bout 'im so much. But de ham had be'n on his neck so long dat Dave had sorter got use' ter it. He look des lack he'd los' sump'n fer a day er so atter de ham wuz tuk off, en didn' 'pear ter know w'at ter do wid hisse'f; en fine'ly he up' 'n' tuk 'n' tied a lighterd-knot ter a string, en hid it under de flo' er his cabin, en w'en nobody wuzn' lookin' he'd take it out en hang it roun' his neck, en go off in de woods en holler en sing; en he alluz tied it roun' his neck w'en he went ter sleep. Fac', it 'peared Dave done gone clean out'n his mine. En atter a w'ile he got one er de quarest notions you eber hearn tell un. It wuz 'bout dat time dat I come back ter de plantation fer ter wuk—I had be'n out ter Mars Dugal's yuther place on Beaver Crick fer a mont' er so. I had hearn 'bout Dave en de bacon, en 'bout w'at wuz gwine on on de plantation; but I didn' b'lieve w'at dey all say 'bout Dave, fer I knowed Dave wa'n't dat kine er man. One day atter I come back, me'n Dave wuz choppin' cotton tergedder, w'en Dave lean' on his hoe, en motion' fer me ter come ober close ter 'im; en den he retch' ober en w'ispered ter me.

"'Julius,' sezee, 'did yer knowed yer wuz wukkin' 'long yer wid a ham?'

"I couldn' 'magine w'at he meant. 'G'way fum yer, Dave,' says I. 'Yer ain' wearin' no ham no mo'; try en fergit 'bout dat; 't ain' gwine ter do yer no good fer ter 'member it.'

"'Look a-year, Julius,' sezee, 'kin yer keep a secret?'

"'Co'se I kin, Dave,' says I. 'I doan go roun' tellin' people w'at yuther folks says ter me.'

"'Kin I trus' yer, Julius? Will yer cross yo' heart?'

"I cross my heart. 'Wush I may die ef I tells a soul,' says I.

"Dave look at me des lack he wuz lookin' thoo me en 'way on de yuther side er me, en sezee:

"'Did yer knowed I wuz turnin' ter a ham, Julius?'

"I tried ter 'suade Dave dat dat wuz all foolishness, en dat he oughtn' ter be talkin' dat-a-way—hit wa'n't right. En I tole 'im ef he'd des be patien', de time would sho'ly come w'en eve'thing would be straighten' out, en folks would fine out who de rale rogue wuz w'at stole de bacon. Dave 'peared ter listen ter w'at I say, en promise' ter do better, en stop gwine on dat-a-way; en it seem lack he pick' up a bit w'en he seed dey wuz one pusson didn' b'lieve dem tales 'bout 'im.

"Hit wa'n't long atter dat befo' Mars Archie McIntyre, ober on de Wim'l'ton road, 'mence' ter complain 'bout somebody stealin' chickens fum his hen-'ouse. De chickens kep' on gwine, en at las' Mars Archie tole de han's on his plantation dat he gwine ter shoot de fus' man he ketch in his hen-'ouse. In less'n a week atter he gin dis warnin', he cotch a nigger in de hen-'ouse, en fill' 'im full er squir'l-shot. W'en he got a light, he 'skivered it wuz a strange nigger; en w'en he call' one er his own sarven's, de nigger tole 'im it wuz our Wiley. W'en Mars Archie foun' dat out, he sont ober ter our plantation fer ter tell Mars Dugal' he had shot one er his niggers, en dat he could sen' ober dere en git w'at wuz lef' un 'im.

"Mars Dugal' wuz mad at fus'; but w'en he got ober dere an hearn how it all happen', he didn' hab much ter say. Wiley wuz shot so bad he wuz sho' he wuz gwine ter die, so he up'n says ter ole marster:

"'Mars Dugal',' sezee, 'I knows I's be'n a monst'us bad nigger, but befo' I go I wanter git sump'n off'n my mine. Dave didn' steal dat bacon w'at wuz tuk out'n de smoke-'ouse. I stole it all, en I hid de ham under Dave's cabin fer ter th'ow de blame on him—en may de good Lawd fergib me fer it.'

"Mars Dugal' had Wiley tuk back ter de plantation, en sont fer a doctor fer ter pick de shot out'n 'im. En de ve'y nex' mawnin' Mars Dugal' sont fer Dave ter come up ter de big house; he felt kinder sorry fer de way Dave had be'n treated. Co'se it wa'n't no fault er Mars Dugal's but he wuz gwine ter do w'at he could fer ter make up fer it. So he sont word down ter de quarters fer Dave en all de yuther han's ter 'semble up in de yard befo' de big house at sun-up nex' mawnin'.

"Yearly in de mawnin' de niggers all swarm' up in de yard. Mars Dugal' wuz feelin' so kine dat he had brung up a bairl er cider, en tole de niggers all fer ter he'p deyselves.

"All de han's on de plantation come but Dave; en bimeby, w'en it seem lack he wa'n't comin', Mars Dugal' sont a nigger down ter de quarters ter look fer 'im. De sun wuz gittin' up, en dey wuz a heap er wuk ter be done, en Mars Dugal' sorter got ti'ed waitin'; so he up'n says:

"'Well, boys en gals, I sont fer yer all up yer fer ter tell yer dat all dat 'bout Dave's stealin' er de bacon wuz a mistake, ez I s'pose yer all done hearn befo' now, en I's mighty sorry it happen'. I wants ter treat all my niggers right, en I wants yer all ter know dat I sets a heap by all er my han's w'at is hones' en smart. En I want yer all ter treat Dave des lack yer did befo' dis thing happen', en mine w'at he preach ter yer; for Dave is a good nigger, en has had a hard row ter hoe. En de fus' one I ketch sayin' anythin' 'g'in' Dave, I'll tell Mister Walker ter gin 'im forty. Now take ernudder drink er cider all roun', en den git at dat cotton, fer I wanter git dat Persimmon Hill trac' all pick' ober ter-day.'

"W'en de niggers wuz gwine 'way, Mars Dugal' tole me fer ter go en hunt up Dave, en bring 'im up ter de house. I went down ter Dave's cabin, but couldn' fine 'im dere. Den I look' roun' de plantation en in de aidge er de woods, en 'long de road; but I couldn' fine no sign er Dave. I wuz 'bout ter gin up de sarch, w'en I happen' fer ter run 'cross a foot-track w'at look' lack Dave's. I has wukked 'long wid Dave so much dat I knowed his tracks: he had a monst'us long foot, wid a holler instep, w'ich wuz sump'n skase 'mongs' black folks. So I followed dat track 'cross de fiel' fum de quarters 'tel I got ter de smoke-'ouse. De fus' thing I notice' wuz smoke comin' out'n de cracks: it wuz cu'ous, caze dey hadn' be'n no hogs kill' on de plantation fer six mont' er so, en all de bacon in de smoke-'ouse wuz done kyoed. I couldn' 'magine fer ter sabe my life w'at Dave wuz doin' in dat smoke-'ouse. I went up ter de do' en hollered:

"'Dave!'

"Dey didn' nobody answer. I didn' wanter open de do', fer w'ite folks is monst'us pertickler 'bout dey smoke-'ouses; en ef de oberseah had a-come up en cotch me in dere, he mou't not wanter b'lieve I wuz des lookin' fer Dave. So I sorter knock at de do' en call' out ag'in:

"'O Dave, hit's me—Julius! Doan be skeered. Mars Dugal' wants yer ter come up ter de big house—he done 'skivered who stole de ham.'

"But Dave didn' answer. En w'en I look' roun' ag'in en didn' seed none er his tracks gwine way fum de smoke-'ouse, I knowed he wuz in dere yit, en I wuz 'termine' fer ter fetch 'im out; so I push de do' open en look in.

"Dey wuz a pile er bark burnin' in de middle er de flo', en right ober de fier, hangin' fum one er de rafters, wuz Dave; dey wuz a rope roun' his neck, en I didn' haf ter look at his face mo' d'n once fer ter see he wuz dead.

"Den I knowed how it all happen'. Dave had kep' on gittin' wusser en wusser in his mine, 'tel he des got ter b'lievin' he wuz all done turnt ter a ham, en den he had gone en built a fier, en tied a rope roun' his neck, des lack de hams wuz tied, en had hung hisse'f up in de smoke-'ouse fer ter kyo.

"Dave wuz buried down by de swamp, in de plantation buryin'-groun'. Wiley didn' died fum de woun' he got in Mars McIntyre's hen-'ouse; he got well atter a w'ile, but Dilsey wouldn' hab nuffin mo' ter do wid 'im, en 't wa'n't long 'fo' Mars Dugal' sol' 'im ter a speki-later on his way souf—he say he didn' want no sich a nigger on de plantation, ner in de county, ef he could he'p it. En w'en de een' er de year come, Mars Dugal' turnt Mars Walker off, en run de plantation hisse'f atter dat.

"Eber sence den," said Julius in conclusion, "w'eneber I eats ham, it min's me er Dave. I lacks ham, but I nebber kin eat mo' d'n two er th'ee poun's befo' I gits ter studyin' 'bout Dave, en den I has ter stop en leab de res' fer ernudder time."

There was a short silence after the old man had finished his story, and then my wife began to talk about the weather, on which subject he was an authority. I went into the house. When I came out, half an hour later, I saw Julius disappearing down the lane, with a basket on his arm.

At breakfast, next morning, it occurred to me that I should like a slice of ham. I said as much to my wife.

"Oh, no, John," she responded, "you shouldn't eat anything so heavy for breakfast."

I insisted.

"The fact is," she said, pensively, "I couldn't have eaten any more of that ham, and I gave it to Julius."

THE SHERIFF'S CHILDREN

BRANSON COUNTY, North Carolina, is in a sequestered district of one of the staidest and most conservative States of the Union. Society in Branson County is almost primitive in its simplicity. Most of the white people own the farms they till, and even before the war there were no very wealthy families to force their neighbors, by comparison, into the category of "poor whites."

To Branson County, as to most rural communities in the South, the war is the one historical event that overshadows all others. It is the era from which all local chronicles are dated,—births, deaths, marriages, storms, freshets. No description of the life of any Southern community would be perfect that failed to emphasize the all pervading influence of the great conflict.

Yet the fierce tide of war that had rushed through the cities and along the great highways of the country had comparatively speaking but slightly disturbed the sluggish current of life in this region, remote from railroads and navigable streams. To the north in Virginia, to the west in Tennessee, and all along the seaboard the war had raged; but the thunder of its cannon had not disturbed the echoes of Branson County, where the loudest sounds heard were the crack of some hunter's rifle, the baying of some deep-mouthed hound, or the yodel of some tuneful negro on his way through the pine forest. To the east, Sherman's army had passed on its march to the sea; but no straggling band of "bummers" had penetrated the confines of Branson County. The war, it is true, had robbed the county of the flower of its young manhood; but the burden of taxation, the doubt and uncertainty of the conflict, and the sting of ultimate defeat, had been borne by the people with an apathy that robbed misfortune of half its sharpness.

The nearest approach to town life afforded by Branson County is found in the little village of Troy, the county seat, a hamlet with a population of four or five hundred.

Ten years make little difference in the appearance of these remote Southern towns. If a railroad is built through one of them, it infuses some enterprise; the social corpse is galvanized by the fresh blood of civilization that pulses along the farthest ramifications of our great system of commercial highways. At the period of which I write, no railroad had come to Troy. If a traveler, accustomed to the bustling life of cities, could have ridden through Troy on a summer day, he might easily have fancied himself in a deserted village. Around him he would have seen weather-beaten houses, innocent of paint, the shingled roofs in many instances covered with a rich growth of moss. Here and there he would have met a razor-backed hog lazily rooting his way along the principal thoroughfare; and more than once he would probably have had to disturb the slumbers of some yellow dog, dozing away the hours in the ardent sunshine, and reluctantly yielding up his place in the middle of the dusty road.

On Saturdays the village presented a somewhat livelier appearance, and the shade trees around the court-house square and along Front Street served as hitching-posts for a goodly number of horses and mules and stunted oxen, belonging to the farmer-folk who had come in to trade at the two or three local stores.

A murder was a rare event in Branson County. Every well-informed citizen could tell the number of homicides committed in the county for fifty years back, and whether the slayer, in any given instance, had escaped, either by flight or acquittal, or had suffered the penalty of the law. So, when it became known in Troy early one Friday morning in summer, about ten years after the war, that old Captain Walker, who had served in Mexico under Scott, and had left an arm on the field of Gettysburg, had been foully murdered during the night, there was intense excitement in the village. Business was practically suspended, and the citizens gathered in little groups to discuss the murder, and speculate upon the identity of the murderer. It transpired from testimony at the coroner's inquest, held during the morning, that a strange mulatto had been seen going in the direction of Captain Walker's house the night before, and had been met going away from Troy early Friday morning, by a farmer on his way to town. Other circumstances seemed to connect the stranger with the crime. The sheriff organized a posse to search for him, and early in the evening, when most of the citizens of Troy were at supper, the suspected man was brought in and lodged in the county jail.

By the following morning the news of the capture had spread to the farthest limits of the county. A much larger number of people than usual came to town that Saturday,—bearded men in straw hats and blue homespun shirts, and butternut trousers of great amplitude of material and vagueness of outline; women in homespun frocks and slat-bonnets, with faces as expressionless as the dreary sand-hills which gave them a meagre sustenance.

The murder was almost the sole topic of conversation. A steady stream of curious observers visited the house of mourning, and gazed upon the rugged face of the old veteran, now stiff and cold in death; and more than one eye dropped a tear at the remembrance of the cheery smile, and the joke—sometimes superannuated, generally feeble, but always good-natured—with which the captain had been wont to greet his acquaintances. There was a growing sentiment of anger among these stern men, toward the murderer who had thus cut down their friend, and a strong feeling that ordinary justice was too slight a punishment for such a crime.

Toward noon there was an informal gathering of citizens in Dan Tyson's store.

"I hear it 'lowed that Square Kyahtah's too sick ter hol' co'te this evenin'," said one, "an' that the purlim'nary hearin' 'll haf ter go over 'tel nex' week."

A look of disappointment went round the crowd.

"Hit 's the durndes', meanes' murder ever committed in this caounty," said another, with moody emphasis.

"I s'pose the nigger 'lowed the Cap'n had some greenbacks," observed a third speaker.

"The Cap'n," said another, with an air of superior information, "has left two bairls of Confedrit money, which he 'spected 'ud be good some day er nuther."

This statement gave rise to a discussion of the speculative value of Confederate money; but in a little while the conversation returned to the murder.

"Hangin' air too good fer the murderer," said one; "he oughter be burnt, stidier bein' hung."

There was an impressive pause at this point, during which a jug of moonlight whiskey went the round of the crowd.

"Well," said a round-shouldered farmer, who, in spite of his peaceable expression and faded gray eye, was known to have been one of the most daring followers of a rebel guerrilla chieftain, "what air yer gwine ter do about it? Ef you fellers air gwine ter set down an' let a wuthless nigger kill the bes' white man in Branson, an' not say nuthin' ner do nuthin', *I'll* move outen the caounty."

This speech gave tone and direction to the rest of the conversation. Whether the fear of losing the round-shouldered farmer operated to bring about the result or not is immaterial to this narrative; but, at all events, the crowd decided to lynch the negro. They agreed that this was the least that could be done to avenge the death of their murdered friend, and that it was a becoming way in which to honor his memory. They had some vague notions of the majesty of the law and the rights of the citizen, but in the passion of the moment these sunk into oblivion; a white man had been killed by a negro.

"The Cap'n was an ole sodger," said one of his friends solemnly. "He'll sleep better when he knows that a co'te-martial has be'n hilt an' jestice done."

By agreement the lynchers were to meet at Tyson's store at five o'clock in the afternoon, and proceed thence to the jail, which was situated down the Lumberton Dirt Road (as the old turnpike antedating the plank-road was called), about half a mile south of the court-house. When the preliminaries of the lynching had been arranged, and a committee appointed to manage the affair, the crowd dispersed, some to go to their dinners, and some to secure recruits for the lynching party.

It was twenty minutes to five o'clock, when an excited negro, panting and perspiring, rushed up to the back door of Sheriff Campbell's dwelling, which stood at a little distance from the jail and somewhat farther than the latter building from the court-house. A turbaned colored woman came to the door in response to the negro's knock.

"Hoddy, Sis' Nance."

"Hoddy, Brer Sam."

"Is de shurff in?" inquired the negro.

"Yas, Brer Sam, he's eatin' his dinner," was the answer.

"Will yer ax 'im ter step ter de do' a minute, Sis' Nance?"

The woman went into the dining-room, and a moment later the sheriff came to the door. He was a tall, muscular man, of a ruddier complexion than is usual among Southerners. A pair of keen, deep-set gray eyes looked out from under bushy eyebrows, and about his mouth was a masterful expression, which a full beard, once sandy in color, but now profusely sprinkled with gray, could not entirely conceal. The day was hot; the sheriff had discarded his coat and vest, and had his white shirt open at the throat.

"What do you want, Sam?" he inquired of the negro, who stood hat in hand, wiping the moisture from his face with a ragged shirt-sleeve.

"Shurff, dey gwine ter hang de pris'ner w'at's lock' up in de jail. Dey're comin' dis a-way now. I wuz layin' down on a sack er corn down at de sto', behine a pile er flour-bairls, w'en I hearn Doc' Cain en Kunnel Wright talkin' erbout it. I slip' outen de back do', en run here as fas' as I could. I hearn you say down ter de sto' once't dat you wouldn't let nobody take a pris'ner 'way fum you widout walkin' over yo' dead body, en I thought I'd let you know 'fo' dey come, so yer could pertec' de pris'ner."

The sheriff listened calmly, but his face grew firmer, and a determined gleam lit up his gray eyes. His frame grew more erect, and he unconsciously assumed the attitude of a soldier who momentarily expects to meet the enemy face to face.

"Much obliged, Sam," he answered. "I'll protect the prisoner. Who's coming?"

"I dunno who-all *is* comin'," replied the negro. "Dere's Mistah McSwayne, en Doc' Cain, en Maje' McDonal', en Kunnel Wright, en a heap er yuthers. I wuz so skeered I done furgot mo' d'n half un em. I spec' dey mus' be mos' here by dis time, so I'll git outen de way, fer I don' want nobody fer ter think I wuz mix' up in dis business." The negro glanced nervously down the road toward the town, and made a movement as if to go away.

"Won't you have some dinner first?" asked the sheriff.

The negro looked longingly in at the open door, and sniffed the appetizing odor of boiled pork and collards.

"I ain't got no time fer ter tarry, Shurff," he said, "but Sis' Nance mought gin me sump'n I could kyar in my han' en eat on de way."

A moment later Nancy brought him a huge sandwich of split cornpone, with a thick slice of fat bacon inserted between the halves, and a couple of baked yams. The negro hastily replaced his ragged hat on his head, dropped the yams in the pocket of his capacious trousers, and, taking the sandwich in his hand, hurried across the road and disappeared in the woods beyond.

The sheriff reentered the house, and put on his coat and hat. He then took down a double-barreled shotgun and loaded it with buckshot. Filling the chambers of a revolver with fresh cartridges, he slipped it into the pocket of the sack-coat which he wore.

A comely young woman in a calico dress watched these proceedings with anxious surprise.

"Where are you going, father?" she asked. She had not heard the conversation with the negro.

"I am goin' over to the jail," responded the sheriff. "There's a mob comin' this way to lynch the nigger we've got locked up. But they won't do it," he added, with emphasis.

"Oh, father! don't go!" pleaded the girl, clinging to his arm; "they'll shoot you if you don't give him up."

"You never mind me, Polly," said her father reassuringly, as he gently unclasped her hands from his arm. "I'll take care of myself and the prisoner, too. There ain't a man in Branson County that would shoot me. Besides, I have faced fire too often to be scared away from my duty. You keep close in the house," he continued, "and if any one disturbs you just use the old horse-pistol in the top bureau drawer. It's a little old-fashioned, but it did good work a few years ago."

The young girl shuddered at this sanguinary allusion, but made no further objection to her father's departure.

The sheriff of Branson was a man far above the average of the community in wealth, education, and social position. His had been one of the few families in the county that before the war had owned large estates and numerous slaves. He had graduated at the State University at Chapel Hill, and had kept up some acquaintance with current literature and advanced thought. He had traveled some in his youth, and was looked up to in the county as an authority on all subjects connected with the outer world. At first an ardent supporter of the Union, he had opposed the secession movement in his native State as long as opposition availed to stem the tide of public opinion. Yielding at last to the force of circumstances, he had entered the Confederate service rather late in the war, and served with distinction through several campaigns, rising in time to the rank of colonel. After the war he had taken the oath of allegiance, and had been chosen by the people as the most available candidate for the office of sheriff, to which he had been elected without opposition. He had filled the office for several terms, and was universally popular with his constituents.

Colonel or Sheriff Campbell, as he was indifferently called, as the military or civil title happened to be most important in the opinion of the person addressing him, had a high sense of the responsibility attaching to his office. He had sworn to do his duty faithfully, and he knew what his duty was, as sheriff, perhaps more clearly than he had apprehended it in other passages of his life. It was, therefore, with no uncertainty in regard to his course that he prepared his weapons and went over to the jail. He had no fears for Polly's safety.

The sheriff had just locked the heavy front door of the jail behind him when a half dozen horsemen, followed by a crowd of men on foot, came round a bend in the road and drew near the jail. They halted in front of the picket fence that surrounded the building, while several of the committee of arrangements rode on a few rods farther to the sheriff's house. One of them dismounted and rapped on the door with his riding-whip.

"Is the sheriff at home?" he inquired.

"No, he has just gone out," replied Polly, who had come to the door.

"We want the jail keys," he continued.

"They are not here," said Polly. "The sheriff has them himself." Then she added, with assumed indifference, "He is at the jail now."

The man turned away, and Polly went into the front room, from which she peered anxiously between the slats of the green blinds of a window that looked toward the jail. Meanwhile the messenger returned to his companions and announced his discovery. It looked as though the sheriff had learned of their design and was preparing to resist it.

One of them stepped forward and rapped on the jail door.

"Well, what is it?" said the sheriff, from within.

"We want to talk to you, Sheriff," replied the spokesman.

There was a little wicket in the door; this the sheriff opened, and answered through it.

"All right, boys, talk away. You are all strangers to me, and I don't know what business you can have." The sheriff did not think it necessary to recognize anybody in particular on such an occasion; the question of identity sometimes comes up in the investigation of these extra-judicial executions.

"We're a committee of citizens and we want to get into the jail."

"What for? It ain't much trouble to get into jail. Most people want to keep out."

The mob was in no humor to appreciate a joke, and the sheriff's witticism fell dead upon an unresponsive audience.

"We want to have a talk with the nigger that killed Cap'n Walker."

"You can talk to that nigger in the court-house, when he's brought out for trial. Court will be in session here next week. I know what you fellows want, but you can't get my prisoner to-day. Do you want to take the bread out of a poor man's mouth? I get seventy-five cents a day for keeping this prisoner, and he's the only one in jail. I can't have my family suffer just to please you fellows."

One or two young men in the crowd laughed at the idea of Sheriff Campbell's suffering for want of seventy-five cents a day; but they were frowned into silence by those who stood near them.

"Ef yer don't let us in," cried a voice, "we'll bu's' the do' open."

"Bust away," answered the sheriff, raising his voice so that all could hear. "But I give you fair warning. The first man that tries it will be filled with buckshot. I'm sheriff of this county; I know my duty, and I mean to do it."

"What's the use of kicking, Sheriff?" argued one of the leaders of the mob. "The nigger is sure to hang anyhow; he richly deserves it; and we've got to do something to teach the niggers their places, or white people won't be able to live in the county."

"There's no use talking, boys," responded the sheriff. "I'm a white man outside, but in this jail I'm sheriff; and if this nigger's to be hung in this county, I propose to do the hanging. So you fellows might as well right-about-face, and march back to Troy. You've had a pleasant trip,

and the exercise will be good for you. You know *me*. I've got powder
and ball, and I've faced fire before now, with nothing between me and
the enemy, and I don't mean to surrender this jail while I'm able to
shoot." Having thus announced his determination, the sheriff closed
and fastened the wicket, and looked around for the best position from
which to defend the building.

The crowd drew off a little, and the leaders conversed together in
low tones.

The Branson County jail was a small, two-story brick building,
strongly constructed, with no attempt at architectural ornamentation.
Each story was divided into two large cells by a passage running from
front to rear. A grated iron door gave entrance from the passage to each
of the four cells. The jail seldom had many prisoners in it, and the
lower windows had been boarded up. When the sheriff had closed the
wicket, he ascended the steep wooden stairs to the upper floor. There
was no window at the front of the upper passage, and the most available
position from which to watch the movements of the crowd below was
the front window of the cell occupied by the solitary prisoner.

The sheriff unlocked the door and entered the cell. The prisoner was
crouched in a corner, his yellow face, blanched with terror, looking
ghastly in the semi-darkness of the room. A cold perspiration had gathered on his forehead, and his teeth were chattering with affright.

"For God's sake, Sheriff," he murmured hoarsely, "don't let 'em
lynch me; I didn't kill the old man."

The sheriff glanced at the cowering wretch with a look of mingled
contempt and loathing.

"Get up," he said sharply. "You will probably be hung sooner or later,
but it shall not be to-day, if I can help it. I'll unlock your fetters, and if
I can't hold the jail, you'll have to make the best fight you can. If I'm
shot, I'll consider my responsibility at an end."

There were iron fetters on the prisoner's ankles, and handcuffs on his
wrists. These the sheriff unlocked, and they fell clanking to the floor.

"Keep back from the window," said the sheriff. "They might shoot if
they saw you."

The sheriff drew toward the window a pine bench which formed a
part of the scanty furniture of the cell, and laid his revolver upon it.
Then he took his gun in hand, and took his stand at the side of the
window where he could with least exposure of himself watch the movements of the crowd below.

The lynchers had not anticipated any determined resistance. Of
course they had looked for a formal protest, and perhaps a sufficient
show of opposition to excuse the sheriff in the eye of any stickler for
legal formalities. They had not, however, come prepared to fight a battle,

and no one of them seemed willing to lead an attack upon the jail. The leaders of the party conferred together with a good deal of animated gesticulation, which was visible to the sheriff from his outlook, though the distance was too great for him to hear what was said. At length one of them broke away from the group, and rode back to the main body of the lynchers, who were restlessly awaiting orders.

"Well, boys," said the messenger, "we'll have to let it go for the present. The sheriff says he'll shoot, and he's got the drop on us this time. There ain't any of us that want to follow Cap'n Walker jest yet. Besides, the sheriff is a good fellow, and we don't want to hurt 'im. But," he added, as if to reassure the crowd, which began to show signs of disappointment, "the nigger might as well say his prayers, for he ain't got long to live."

There was a murmur of dissent from the mob, and several voices insisted that an attack be made on the jail. But pacific counsels finally prevailed, and the mob sullenly withdrew.

The sheriff stood at the window until they had disappeared around the bend in the road. He did not relax his watchfulness when the last one was out of sight. Their withdrawal might be a mere feint, to be followed by a further attempt. So closely, indeed, was his attention drawn to the outside, that he neither saw nor heard the prisoner creep stealthily across the floor, reach out his hand and secure the revolver which lay on the bench behind the sheriff, and creep as noiselessly back to his place in the corner of the room.

A moment after the last of the lynching party had disappeared there was a shot fired from the woods across the road; a bullet whistled by the window and buried itself in the wooden casing a few inches from where the sheriff was standing. Quick as thought, with the instinct born of a semi-guerrilla army experience, he raised his gun and fired twice at the point from which a faint puff of smoke showed the hostile bullet to have been sent. He stood a moment watching, and then rested his gun against the window, and reached behind him mechanically for the other weapon. It was not on the bench. As the sheriff realized this fact, he turned his head and looked into the muzzle of the revolver.

"Stay where you are, Sheriff," said the prisoner, his eyes glistening, his face almost ruddy with excitement.

The sheriff mentally cursed his own carelessness for allowing him to be caught in such a predicament. He had not expected anything of the kind. He had relied on the negro's cowardice and subordination in the presence of an armed white man as a matter of course. The sheriff was a brave man, but realized that the prisoner had him at an immense disadvantage. The two men stood thus for a moment, fighting a harmless duel with their eyes.

"Well, what do you mean to do?" asked the sheriff with apparent calmness.

"To get away, of course," said the prisoner, in a tone which caused the sheriff to look at him more closely, and with an involuntary feeling of apprehension; if the man was not mad, he was in a state of mind akin to madness, and quite as dangerous. The sheriff felt that he must speak the prisoner fair, and watch for a chance to turn the tables on him. The keen-eyed, desperate man before him was a different being altogether from the groveling wretch who had begged so piteously for life a few minutes before.

At length the sheriff spoke: —

"Is this your gratitude to me for saving your life at the risk of my own? If I had not done so, you would now be swinging from the limb of some neighboring tree."

"True," said the prisoner, "you saved my life, but for how long? When you came in, you said Court would sit next week. When the crowd went away they said I had not long to live. It is merely a choice of two ropes."

"While there's life there's hope," replied the sheriff. He uttered this commonplace mechanically, while his brain was busy in trying to think out some way of escape. "If you are innocent you can prove it."

The mulatto kept his eye upon the sheriff. "I didn't kill the old man," he replied; "but I shall never be able to clear myself. I was at his house at nine o'clock. I stole from it the coat that was on my back when I was taken. I would be convicted, even with a fair trial, unless the real murderer were discovered beforehand."

The sheriff knew this only too well. While he was thinking what argument next to use, the prisoner continued: —

"Throw me the keys — no, unlock the door."

The sheriff stood a moment irresolute. The mulatto's eye glittered ominously. The sheriff crossed the room and unlocked the door leading into the passage.

"Now go down and unlock the outside door."

The heart of the sheriff leaped within him. Perhaps he might make a dash for liberty, and gain the outside. He descended the narrow stairs, the prisoner keeping close behind him.

The sheriff inserted the huge iron key into the lock. The rusty bolt yielded slowly. It still remained for him to pull the door open.

"Stop!" thundered the mulatto, who seemed to divine the sheriff's purpose. "Move a muscle, and I'll blow your brains out."

The sheriff obeyed; he realized that his chance had not yet come.

"Now keep on that side of the passage, and go back upstairs."

Keeping the sheriff under cover of the revolver, the mulatto followed him up the stairs. The sheriff expected the prisoner to lock him into the cell and make his own escape. He had about come to the conclusion that the best thing he could do under the circumstances was to submit quietly, and take his chances of recapturing the prisoner after the alarm had been given. The sheriff had faced death more than once upon the battlefield. A few minutes before, well armed, and with a brick wall between him and them, he had dared a hundred men to fight; but he felt instinctively that the desperate man confronting him was not to be trifled with, and he was too prudent a man to risk his life against such heavy odds. He had Polly to look after, and there was a limit beyond which devotion to duty would be quixotic and even foolish.

"I want to get away," said the prisoner, "and I don't want to be captured; for if I am I know I will be hung on the spot. I am afraid," he added somewhat reflectively, "that in order to save myself I shall have to kill you."

"Good God!" exclaimed the sheriff in involuntary terror; "you would not kill the man to whom you owe your own life."

"You speak more truly than you know," replied the mulatto. "I indeed owe my life to you."

The sheriff started. He was capable of surprise, even in that moment of extreme peril. "Who are you?" he asked in amazement.

"Tom, Cicely's son," returned the other. He had closed the door and stood talking to the sheriff through the grated opening. "Don't you remember Cicely—Cicely whom you sold, with her child, to the speculator on his way to Alabama?"

The sheriff did remember. He had been sorry for it many a time since. It had been the old story of debts, mortgages, and bad crops. He had quarreled with the mother. The price offered for her and her child had been unusually large, and he had yielded to the combination of anger and pecuniary stress.

"Good God!" he gasped, "you would not murder your own father?"

"My father?" replied the mulatto. "It were well enough for me to claim the relationship, but it comes with poor grace from you to ask anything by reason of it. What father's duty have you ever performed for me? Did you give me your name, or even your protection? Other white men gave their colored sons freedom and money, and sent them to the free States. You sold *me* to the rice swamps."

"I at least gave you the life you cling to," murmured the sheriff.

"Life?" said the prisoner, with a sarcastic laugh. "What kind of a life? You gave me your own blood, your own features,—no man need look at us together twice to see that,—and you gave me a black mother. Poor wretch! She died under the lash, because she had enough womanhood to call her soul her own. You gave me a white man's spirit, and you made me a slave, and crushed it out."

"But you are free now," said the sheriff. He had not doubted, could not doubt, the mulatto's word. He knew whose passions coursed beneath that swarthy skin and burned in the black eyes opposite his own. He saw in this mulatto what he himself might have become had not the safe-guards of parental restraint and public opinion been thrown around him.

"Free to do what?" replied the mulatto. "Free in name, but despised and scorned and set aside by the people to whose race I belong far more than to my mother's."

"There are schools," said the sheriff. "You have been to school." He had noticed that the mulatto spoke more eloquently and used better language than most Branson County people.

"I have been to school, and dreamed when I went that it would work some marvelous change in my condition. But what did I learn? I learned to feel that no degree of learning or wisdom will change the color of my skin and that I shall always wear what in my own country is a badge of degradation. When I think about it seriously I do not care particularly for such a life. It is the animal in me, not the man, that flees the gallows. I owe you nothing," he went on, "and expect nothing of you; and it would be no more than justice if I should avenge upon you my mother's wrongs and my own. But still I hate to shoot you; I have never yet taken human life—for I did *not* kill the old captain. Will you promise to give no alarm and make no attempt to capture me until morning, if I do not shoot?"

So absorbed were the two men in their colloquy and their own tumultuous thoughts that neither of them had heard the door below move upon its hinges. Neither of them had heard a light step come stealthily up the stairs, nor seen a slender form creep along the dark-ening passage toward the mulatto.

The sheriff hesitated. The struggle between his love of life and his sense of duty was a terrific one. It may seem strange that a man who could sell his own child into slavery should hesitate at such a moment, when his life was trembling in the balance. But the baleful influence of human slavery poisoned the very fountains of life, and created new standards of right. The sheriff was conscientious; his conscience had merely been warped by his environment. Let no one ask what his answer would have been; he was spared the necessity of a decision.

"Stop," said the mulatto, "you need not promise. I could not trust you if you did. It is your life for mine; there is but one safe way for me; you must die."

He raised his arm to fire, when there was a flash—a report from the passage behind him. His arm fell heavily at his side, and the pistol dropped at his feet.

The sheriff recovered first from his surprise, and throwing open the door secured the fallen weapon. Then seizing the prisoner he thrust him into the cell and locked the door upon him; after which he turned to Polly, who leaned half-fainting against the wall, her hands clasped over her heart.

"Oh, father, I was just in time," she cried hysterically, and, wildly sobbing, threw herself into her father's arms.

"I watched until they all went away," she said. "I heard the shot from the woods and I saw you shoot. Then when you did not come out I feared something had happened, that perhaps you had been wounded. I got out the other pistol and ran over here. When I found the door open, I knew something was wrong, and when I heard voices I crept upstairs, and reached the top just in time to hear him say he would kill you. Oh, it was a narrow escape!"

When she had grown somewhat calmer, the sheriff left her standing there and went back into the cell. The prisoner's arm was bleeding from a flesh wound. His bravado had given place to a stony apathy. There was no sign in his face of fear or disappointment or feeling of any kind. The sheriff sent Polly to the house for cloth, and bound up the prisoner's wound with a rude skill acquired during his army life.

"I'll have a doctor come and dress the wound in the morning," he said to the prisoner. "It will do very well until then, if you will keep quiet. If the doctor asks you how the wound was caused, you can say that you were struck by the bullet fired from the woods. It would do you no good to have it known that you were shot while attempting to escape."

The prisoner uttered no word of thanks or apology, but sat in sullen silence. When the wounded arm had been bandaged, Polly and her father returned to the house.

The sheriff was in an unusually thoughtful mood that evening. He put salt in his coffee at supper, and poured vinegar over his pancakes. To many of Polly's questions he returned random answers. When he had gone to bed he lay awake for several hours.

In the silent watches of the night, when he was alone with God, there came into his mind a flood of unaccustomed thoughts. An hour or two before, standing face to face with death, he had experienced a sensation similar to that which drowning men are said to feel—a kind of clarifying of the moral faculty, in which the veil of the flesh, and its obscuring passions and prejudices, is pushed aside for a moment, and all the acts of one's life stand out, in the clear light of truth, in their correct proportions and relations,—a state of mind in which one sees himself as God may be supposed to see him. In the reaction following his rescue, this feeling had given place for a time to far different emotions. But now, in the silence of midnight, something of this clearness of spirit returned to the sheriff. He saw that he had owed some duty to this son of his,—that neither law nor custom could destroy a responsibility inherent in the nature of mankind. He could not thus, in the eyes of God at least, shake off the consequences of his sin. Had he never sinned, this wayward spirit would never have come back from the vanished past to haunt him. As these thoughts came, his anger against the mulatto died away, and in its place there sprang up a great pity. The hand of parental authority might have restrained the passions he had seen burning in the prisoner's eyes when the desperate man spoke the words which had seemed to doom his father to death. The sheriff felt that he might have saved this fiery spirit from the slough of slavery; that he might have sent him to the free North, and given him there, or in some other land, an opportunity to turn to usefulness and honorable pursuits the talents that had run to crime, perhaps to madness; he might, still less, have given this son of his the poor simulacrum of liberty which men of his caste could possess in a slave-holding community; or least of all, but still something, he might have kept the boy on the plantation, where the burdens of slavery would have fallen lightly upon him.

The sheriff recalled his own youth. He had inherited an honored name to keep untarnished; he had had a future to make; the picture of a fair young bride had beckoned him on to happiness. The poor wretch now stretched upon a pallet of straw between the brick walls of the jail had had none of these things,—no name, no father, no mother—in the true meaning of motherhood,—and until the past few years no possible future, and then one vague and shadowy in its outline, and dependent for form and substance upon the slow solution of a problem in which there were many unknown quantities.

From what he might have done to what he might yet do was an easy transition for the awakened conscience of the sheriff. It occurred to him, purely as a hypothesis, that he might permit his prisoner to escape; but his oath of office, his duty as sheriff, stood in the way of such a course, and the sheriff dismissed the idea from his mind. He could, however, investigate the circumstances of the murder, and move Heaven and earth to discover the real criminal, for he no longer doubted the prisoner's innocence; he could employ counsel for the accused, and perhaps influence public opinion in his favor. An acquittal once secured, some plan could be devised by which the sheriff might in some degree atone for his crime against this son of his—against society—against God.

When the sheriff had reached this conclusion he fell into an unquiet slumber, from which he awoke late the next morning.

He went over to the jail before breakfast and found the prisoner lying on his pallet, his face turned to the wall; he did not move when the sheriff rattled the door.

"Good-morning," said the latter, in a tone intended to waken the prisoner.

There was no response. The sheriff looked more keenly at the recumbent figure; there was an unnatural rigidity about its attitude.

He hastily unlocked the door and, entering the cell, bent over the prostrate form. There was no sound of breathing; he turned the body over—it was cold and stiff. The prisoner had torn the bandage from his wound and bled to death during the night. He had evidently been dead several hours.

THE WIFE OF HIS YOUTH

I

MR. RYDER was going to give a ball. There were several reasons why
this was an opportune time for such an event.

Mr. Ryder might aptly be called the dean of the Blue Veins. The
original Blue Veins were a little society of colored persons organized in
a certain Northern city shortly after the war. Its purpose was to establish and maintain correct social standards among a people whose social
condition presented almost unlimited room for improvement. By accident, combined perhaps with some natural affinity, the society consisted
of individuals who were, generally speaking, more white than black.
Some envious outsider made the suggestion that no one was eligible for
membership who was not white enough to show blue veins. The suggestion was readily adopted by those who were not of the favored few,
and since that time the society, though possessing a longer and more
pretentious name, had been known far and wide as the "Blue Vein
Society," and its members as the "Blue Veins."

The Blue Veins did not allow that any such requirement existed for
admission to their circle, but, on the contrary, declared that character
and culture were the only things considered; and that if most of their
members were light-colored, it was because such persons, as a rule, had
had better opportunities to qualify themselves for membership.
Opinions differed, too, as to the usefulness of the society. There were
those who had been known to assail it violently as a glaring example of
the very prejudice from which the colored race had suffered most; and
later, when such critics had succeeded in getting on the inside, they
had been heard to maintain with zeal and earnestness that the society
was a lifeboat, an anchor, a bulwark and a shield, —a pillar of cloud by
day and of fire by night, to guide their people through the social wilder-
ness. Another alleged prerequisite for Blue Vein membership was that

of free birth; and while there was really no such requirement, it is doubtless true that very few of the members would have been unable to meet it if there had been. If there were one or two of the older members who had come up from the South and from slavery, their history presented enough romantic circumstances to rob their servile origin of its grosser aspects.

While there were no such tests of eligibility, it is true that the Blue Veins had their notions on these subjects, and that not all of them were equally liberal in regard to the things they collectively disclaimed. Mr. Ryder was one of the most conservative. Though he had not been among the founders of the society, but had come in some years later, his genius for social leadership was such that he had speedily become its recognized adviser and head, the custodian of its standards, and the preserver of its traditions. He shaped its social policy, was active in providing for its entertainment, and when the interest fell off, as it sometimes did, he fanned the embers until they burst again into a cheerful flame.

There were still other reasons for his popularity. While he was not as white as some of the Blue Veins, his appearance was such as to confer distinction upon them. His features were of a refined type, his hair was almost straight; he was always neatly dressed; his manners were irreproachable, and his morals above suspicion. He had come to Groveland a young man, and obtaining employment in the office of a railroad company as messenger had in time worked himself up to the position of stationery clerk, having charge of the distribution of the office supplies for the whole company. Although the lack of early training had hindered the orderly development of a naturally fine mind, it had not prevented him from doing a great deal of reading or from forming decidedly literary tastes. Poetry was his passion. He could repeat whole pages of the great English poets; and if his pronunciation was sometimes faulty, his eye, his voice, his gestures, would respond to the changing sentiment with a precision that revealed a poetic soul and disarmed criticism. He was economical, and had saved money; he owned and occupied a very comfortable house on a respectable street. His residence was handsomely furnished, containing among other things a good library, especially rich in poetry, a piano, and some choice engravings. He generally shared his house with some young couple, who looked after his wants and were company for him; for Mr. Ryder was a single man. In the early days of his connection with the Blue Veins he had been regarded as quite a catch, and young ladies and their mothers had manœuvred with much ingenuity to capture him. Not, however, until Mrs. Molly Dixon visited Groveland had any woman ever made him wish to change his condition to that of a married man.

Mrs. Dixon had come to Groveland from Washington in the spring, and before the summer was over she had won Mr. Ryder's heart. She possessed many attractive qualities. She was much younger than he; in fact, he was old enough to have been her father, though no one knew exactly how old he was. She was whiter than he, and better educated. She had moved in the best colored society of the country, at Washington, and had taught in the schools of the city. Such a superior person had been eagerly welcomed to the Blue Vein Society, and had taken a leading part in its activities. Mr. Ryder had at first been attracted by her charms of person, for she was very good looking and not over twenty-five; then by her refined manners and the vivacity of her wit. Her husband had been a government clerk, and at his death had left a considerable life insurance. She was visiting friends in Groveland, and, finding the town and the people to her liking, had prolonged her stay indefinitely. She had not seemed displeased at Mr. Ryder's attentions, but on the contrary had given him every proper encouragement; indeed, a younger and less cautious man would long since have spoken. But he had made up his mind, and had only to determine the time when he would ask her to be his wife. He decided to give a ball in her honor, and at some time during the evening of the ball to offer her his heart and hand. He had no special fears about the outcome, but, with a little touch of romance, he wanted the surroundings to be in harmony with his own feelings when he should have received the answer he expected.

Mr. Ryder resolved that this ball should mark an epoch in the social history of Groveland. He knew, of course,—no one could know better,—the entertainments that had taken place in past years, and what must be done to surpass them. His ball must be worthy of the lady in whose honor it was to be given, and must, by the quality of its guests, set an example for the future. He had observed of late a growing liberality, almost a laxity, in social matters, even among members of his own set, and had several times been forced to meet in a social way persons whose complexions and callings in life were hardly up to the standards which he considered proper for the society to maintain. He had a theory of his own.

"I have no race prejudice," he would say, "but we people of mixed blood are ground between the upper and the nether millstone. Our fate lies between absorption by the white race and extinction in the black. The one doesn't want us yet, but may take us in time. The other would welcome us, but it would be for us a backward step. 'With malice toward none, with charity for all,' we must do the best we can for ourselves and those who are to follow us. Self-preservation is the first law of nature."

His ball would serve by its exclusiveness to counteract leveling tendencies, and his marriage with Mrs. Dixon would help to further the upward process of absorption he had been wishing and waiting for.

II

The ball was to take place on Friday night. The house had been put in order, the carpets covered with canvas, the halls and stairs decorated with palms and potted plants; and in the afternoon Mr. Ryder sat on his front porch, which the shade of a vine running up over a wire netting made a cool and pleasant lounging place. He expected to respond to the toast "The Ladies" at the supper, and from a volume of Tennyson — his favorite poet — was fortifying himself with apt quotations. The volume was open at "A Dream of Fair Women." His eyes fell on these lines, and he read them aloud to judge better of their effect: —

> "At length I saw a lady within call,
>   Stiller than chisell'd marble, standing there;
> A daughter of the gods, divinely tall,
>   And most divinely fair."

He marked the verse, and turning the page read the stanza beginning, —

> "O sweet pale Margaret,
> O rare pale Margaret."

He weighed the passage a moment, and decided that it would not do. Mrs. Dixon was the palest lady he expected at the ball, and she was of a rather ruddy complexion, and of lively disposition and buxom build. So he ran over the leaves until his eye rested on the description of Queen Guinevere: —

> "She seem'd a part of joyous Spring:
> A gown of grass-green silk she wore,
> Buckled with golden clasps before;
> A light-green tuft of plumes she bore
> Closed in a golden ring.

> •   •   •   •   •   •

> "She look'd so lovely, as she sway'd
> The rein with dainty finger-tips,
> A man had given all other bliss,
> And all his worldly worth for this,
> To waste his whole heart in one kiss
> Upon her perfect lips."

As Mr. Ryder murmured these words audibly, with an appreciative thrill, he heard the latch of his gate click, and a light footfall sounding on the steps. He turned his head, and saw a woman standing before his door.

She was a little woman, not five feet tall, and proportioned to her height. Although she stood erect, and looked around her with very bright and restless eyes, she seemed quite old; for her face was crossed and recrossed with a hundred wrinkles, and around the edges of her bonnet could be seen protruding here and there a tuft of short gray wool. She wore a blue calico gown of ancient cut, a little red shawl fastened around her shoulders with an old-fashioned brass brooch, and a large bonnet profusely ornamented with faded red and yellow artificial flowers. And she was very black,—so black that her toothless gums, revealed when she opened her mouth to speak, were not red, but blue. She looked like a bit of the old plantation life, summoned up from the past by the wave of a magician's wand, as the poet's fancy had called into being the gracious shapes of which Mr. Ryder had just been reading.

He rose from his chair and came over to where she stood.

"Good-afternoon, madam," he said.

"Good-evenin', suh," she answered, ducking suddenly with a quaint curtsy. Her voice was shrill and piping, but softened somewhat by age. "Is dis yere whar Mistuh Ryduh lib, suh?" she asked, looking around her doubtfully, and glancing into the open windows, through which some of the preparations for the evening were visible.

"Yes," he replied, with an air of kindly patronage, unconsciously flattered by her manner, "I am Mr. Ryder. Did you want to see me?"

"Yas, suh, ef I ain't 'sturbin' of you too much."

"Not at all. Have a seat over here behind the vine, where it is cool. What can I do for you?"

"'Scuse me, suh," she continued, when she had sat down on the edge of a chair, "'scuse me, suh, I's lookin' for my husban'. I heerd you wuz a big man an' had libbed heah a long time, an' I 'lowed you wouldn't min' ef I'd come roun' an' ax you ef you'd ever heerd of a merlatter man by de name er Sam Taylor 'quirin' roun' in de chu'ches ermongs' de people fer his wife 'Liza Jane?"

Mr. Ryder seemed to think for a moment.

"There used to be many such cases right after the war," he said, "but it has been so long that I have forgotten them. There are very few now. But tell me your story, and it may refresh my memory."

She sat back farther in her chair so as to be more comfortable, and folded her withered hands in her lap.

"My name's 'Liza," she began, "'Liza Jane. W'en I wuz young I us'ter b'long ter Marse Bob Smif, down in ole Missoura. I wuz bawn down dere. W'en I wuz a gal I wuz married ter a man named Jim. But Jim died, an' after dat I married a merlatter man named Sam Taylor.

Sam wuz free-bawn, but his mammy an' daddy died, an' de w'ite folks 'prenticed him ter my marster fer ter work fer 'im 'tel he wuz growed up. Sam worked in de fiel', an' I wuz de cook. One day Ma'y Ann, ole miss's maid, came rushin' out ter de kitchen, an' says she, ''Liza Jane, ole marse gwine sell yo' Sam down de ribber.'

"'Go way f'm yere,' says I; 'my husban's free!'

"'Don' make no diff'ence. I heerd ole marse tell ole miss he wuz gwine take yo' Sam 'way wid 'im ter-morrow, fer he needed money, an' he knowed whar he could git a t'ousan' dollars fer Sam an' no questions axed.'

"W'en Sam come home f'm de fiel' dat night, I tole him 'bout ole marse gwine steal 'im, an' Sam run erway. His time wuz mos' up, an' he swo' dat w'en he wuz twenty-one he would come back an' he'p me run erway, er else save up de money ter buy my freedom. An' I know he'd 'a' done it, fer he thought a heap er me, Sam did. But w'en he come back he didn' fin' me, fer I wuzn' dere. Ole marse had heerd dat I warned Sam, so he had me whip' an' sol' down de ribber.

"Den de wah broke out, an' w'en it wuz ober de cullud folks wuz scattered. I went back ter de ole home; but Sam wuzn' dere, an' I could n' l'arn nuffin' 'bout 'im. But I knowed he'd be'n dere to look fer me an' hadn' foun' me, an' had gone erway ter hunt fer me.

"I's be'n lookin' fer 'im eber sence," she added simply, as though twenty-five years were but a couple of weeks, "an' I knows he's be'n lookin' fer me. Fer he sot a heap er sto' by me, Sam did, an' I know he's be'n huntin' fer me all dese years,—'less'n he's be'n sick er sump'n, so he couldn' work, er out'n his head, so he couldn' 'member his promise. I went back down de ribber, fer I 'lowed he'd gone down dere lookin' fer me. I's be'n ter Noo Orleens, an' Atlanty, an' Charleston, an' Richmon'; an' w'en I'd be'n all ober de Souf I come ter de Norf. Fer I knows I'll fin' 'im some er dese days," she added softly, "er he'll fin' me, an' den we'll bofe be as happy in freedom as we wuz in de ole days befo' de wah." A smile stole over her withered countenance as she paused a moment, and her bright eyes softened into a far-away look.

This was the substance of the old woman's story. She had wandered a little here and there. Mr. Ryder was looking at her curiously when she finished.

"How have you lived all these years?" he asked.

"Cookin', suh. I's a good cook. Does you know anybody w'at needs a good cook, suh? I's stoppin' wid a cullud fam'ly roun' de corner yonder 'tel I kin git a place."

"Do you really expect to find your husband? He may be dead long ago."

She shook her head emphatically. "Oh no, he ain' dead. De signs an' de tokens tells me. I dremp three nights runnin' on'y dis las' week dat I foun' him."

"He may have married another woman. Your slave marriage would not have prevented him, for you never lived with him after the war, and without that your marriage doesn't count."

"Wouldn' make no diff'ence wid Sam. He wouldn' marry no yuther 'oman 'tel he foun' out 'bout me. I knows it," she added. "Sump'n 's be'n tellin' me all dese years dat I's gwine fin' Sam 'fo' I dies."

"Perhaps he's outgrown you, and climbed up in the world where he wouldn't care to have you find him."

"No, indeed, suh," she replied, "Sam ain' dat kin' er man. He wuz good ter me, Sam wuz, but he wuzn' much good ter nobody e'se, fer he wuz one er de triflin'es' han's on de plantation. I 'spec's ter haf ter suppo't 'im w'en I fin' 'im, fer he nebber would work 'less'n he had ter. But den he wuz free, an' he didn' git no pay fer his work, an' I don' blame 'im much. Mebbe he's done better sence he run erway, but I ain' 'spectin' much."

"You may have passed him on the street a hundred times during the twenty-five years, and not have known him; time works great changes."

She smiled incredulously. "I'd know 'im 'mongs' a hund'ed men. Fer dey wuzn' no yuther merlatter man like my man Sam, an' I couldn' be mistook. I's toted his picture roun' wid me twenty-five years."

"May I see it?" asked Mr. Ryder. "It might help me to remember whether I have seen the original."

As she drew a small parcel from her bosom he saw that it was fastened to a string that went around her neck. Removing several wrappers, she brought to light an old-fashioned daguerreotype in a black case. He looked long and intently at the portrait. It was faded with time, but the features were still distinct, and it was easy to see what manner of man it had represented.

He closed the case, and with a slow movement handed it back to her.

"I don't know of any man in town who goes by that name," he said, "nor have I heard of any one making such inquiries. But if you will leave me your address, I will give the matter some attention, and if I find out anything I will let you know."

She gave him the number of a house in the neighborhood, and went away, after thanking him warmly.

He wrote the address on the fly-leaf of the volume of Tennyson, and, when she had gone, rose to his feet and stood looking after her curiously. As she walked down the street with mincing step, he saw several persons whom she passed turn and look back at her with a smile of kindly amusement. When she had turned the corner, he went upstairs to his bedroom, and stood for a long time before the mirror of his dressing-case, gazing thoughtfully at the reflection of his own face.

III

At eight o'clock the ballroom was a blaze of light and the guests had begun to assemble; for there was a literary programme and some routine business of the society to be gone through with before the dancing. A black servant in evening dress waited at the door and directed the guests to the dressing-rooms.

The occasion was long memorable among the colored people of the city; not alone for the dress and display, but for the high average of intelligence and culture that distinguished the gathering as a whole. There were a number of school-teachers, several young doctors, three or four lawyers, some professional singers, an editor, a lieutenant in the United States army spending his furlough in the city, and others in various polite callings; these were colored, though most of them would not have attracted even a casual glance because of any marked difference from white people. Most of the ladies were in evening costume, and dress coats and dancing pumps were the rule among the men. A band of string music, stationed in an alcove behind a row of palms, played popular airs while the guests were gathering.

The dancing began at half past nine. At eleven o'clock supper was served. Mr. Ryder had left the ballroom some little time before the intermission, but reappeared at the supper-table. The spread was worthy of the occasion, and the guests did full justice to it. When the coffee had been served, the toast-master, Mr. Solomon Sadler, rapped for order. He made a brief introductory speech, complimenting host and guests, and then presented in their order the toasts of the evening. They were responded to with a very fair display of after-dinner wit.

"The last toast," said the toast-master, when he reached the end of the list, "is one which must appeal to us all. There is no one of us of the sterner sex who is not at some time dependent upon woman,—in infancy for protection, in manhood for companionship, in old age for care and comforting. Our good host has been trying to live alone, but the fair faces I see around me to-night prove that he too is largely dependent upon the gentler sex for most that makes life worth living,— the society and love of friends,—and rumor is at fault if he does not soon yield entire subjection to one of them. Mr. Ryder will now respond to the toast,—The Ladies."

There was a pensive look in Mr. Ryder's eyes as he took the floor and adjusted his eye-glasses. He began by speaking of woman as the gift of Heaven to man, and after some general observations on the relations of the sexes he said: "But perhaps the quality which most distinguishes woman is her fidelity and devotion to those she loves. History is full of examples, but has recorded none more striking than one which only to-day came under my notice."

He then related, simply but effectively, the story told by his visitor of the afternoon. He gave it in the same soft dialect, which came readily to his lips, while the company listened attentively and sympathetically. For the story had awakened a responsive thrill in many hearts. There were some present who had seen, and others who had heard their fathers and grandfathers tell, the wrongs and sufferings of this past generation, and all of them still felt, in their darker moments, the shadow hanging over them. Mr. Ryder went on: —

"Such devotion and confidence are rare even among women. There are many who would have searched a year, some who would have waited five years, a few who might have hoped ten years; but for twenty-five years this woman has retained her affection for and her faith in a man she has not seen or heard of in all that time.

"She came to me to-day in the hope that I might be able to help her find this long-lost husband. And when she was gone I gave my fancy rein, and imagined a case I will put to you.

"Suppose that this husband, soon after his escape, had learned that his wife had been sold away, and that such inquiries as he could make brought no information of her whereabouts. Suppose that he was young, and she much older than he; that he was light, and she was black; that their marriage was a slave marriage, and legally binding only if they chose to make it so after the war. Suppose, too, that he made his way to the North, as some of us have done, and there, where he had larger opportunities, had improved them, and had in the course of all these years grown to be as different from the ignorant boy who ran away from fear of slavery as the day is from the night. Suppose, even, that he had qualified himself, by industry, by thrift, and by study, to win the friendship and be considered worthy of the society of such people as these I see around me to-night, gracing my board and filling my heart with gladness; for I am old enough to remember the day when such a gathering would not have been possible in this land. Suppose, too, that, as the years went by, this man's memory of the past grew more and more indistinct, until at last it was rarely, except in his dreams, that any image of this bygone period rose before his mind. And then suppose that accident should bring to his knowledge the fact that the wife of his youth, the wife he had left behind him, — not one who had walked by his side and kept pace with him in his upward struggle, but one upon whom advancing years and a laborious life had set their mark, — was alive and seeking him, but that he was absolutely safe from recognition or discovery, unless he chose to reveal himself. My friends, what would the man do? I will presume that he was one who loved honor, and tried to deal justly with all men. I will even carry the case further, and suppose that perhaps he had set his heart upon another, whom he had hoped to call his own. What would he do, or rather what ought he to do, in such a crisis of a lifetime?

"It seemed to me that he might hesitate, and I imagined that I was an old friend, a near friend, and that he had come to me for advice; and I argued the case with him. I tried to discuss it impartially. After we had looked upon the matter from every point of view, I said to him, in the words that we all know: —

> 'This above all: to thine own self be true,
> And it must follow, as the night the day,
> Thou canst not then be false to any man.'

Then, finally, I put the question to him, 'Shall you acknowledge her?'

"And now, ladies and gentlemen, friends and companions, I ask you, what should he have done?"

There was something in Mr. Ryder's voice that stirred the hearts of those who sat around him. It suggested more than mere sympathy with an imaginary situation; it seemed rather in the nature of a personal appeal. It was observed, too, that his look rested more especially upon Mrs. Dixon, with a mingled expression of renunciation and inquiry.

She had listened, with parted lips and streaming eyes. She was the first to speak: "He should have acknowledged her."

"Yes," they all echoed, "he should have acknowledged her."

"My friends and companions," responded Mr. Ryder, "I thank you, one and all. It is the answer I expected, for I knew your hearts."

He turned and walked toward the closed door of an adjoining room, while every eye followed him in wondering curiosity. He came back in a moment, leading by the hand his visitor of the afternoon, who stood startled and trembling at the sudden plunge into this scene of brilliant gayety. She was neatly dressed in gray, and wore the white cap of an elderly woman.

"Ladies and gentlemen," he said, "this is the woman, and I am the man, whose story I have told you. Permit me to introduce to you the wife of my youth."

SIS' BECKY'S PICKANINNY

WE HAD not lived in North Carolina very long before I was able to note a marked improvement in my wife's health. The ozone-laden air of the surrounding piney woods, the mild and equable climate, the peaceful leisure of country life, had brought about in hopeful measure the cure we had anticipated. Toward the end of our second year, however, her ailment took an unexpected turn for the worse. She became the victim of a settled melancholy, attended with vague forebodings of impending misfortune.

"You must keep up her spirits," said our physician, the best in the neighboring town. "This melancholy lowers her tone too much, tends to lessen her strength, and, if it continues too long, may be fraught with grave consequences."

I tried various expedients to cheer her up. I read novels to her. I had the hands on the place come up in the evening and serenade her with plantation songs. Friends came in sometimes and talked, and frequent letters from the North kept her in touch with her former home. But nothing seemed to rouse her from the depression into which she had fallen.

One pleasant afternoon in spring, I placed an armchair in a shaded portion of the front piazza, and filling it with pillows led my wife out of the house and seated her where she would have the pleasantest view of a somewhat monotonous scenery. She was scarcely placed when old Julius came through the yard, and, taking off his tattered straw hat, inquired, somewhat anxiously:—

"How is you feelin' dis afternoon, ma'm?"

"She is not very cheerful, Julius," I said. My wife was apparently without energy enough to speak for herself.

The old man did not seem inclined to go away, so I asked him to sit down. I had noticed, as he came up, that he held some small object in his hand. When he had taken his seat on the top step, he kept fingering this object,—what it was I could not quite make out.

57

"What is that you have there, Julius?" I asked, with mild curiosity.

"Dis is my rabbit foot, suh."

This was at a time before this curious superstition had attained its present jocular popularity among white people, and while I had heard of it before, it had not yet outgrown the charm of novelty.

"What do you do with it?"

"I kyars it wid me fer luck, suh."

"Julius," I observed, half to him and half to my wife, "your people will never rise in the world until they throw off these childish superstitions and learn to live by the light of reason and common sense. How absurd to imagine that the fore-foot of a poor dead rabbit, with which he timorously felt his way along through a life surrounded by snares and pitfalls, beset by enemies on every hand, can promote happiness or success, or ward off failure or misfortune!"

"It is ridiculous," assented my wife, with faint interest.

"Dat's w'at I tells dese niggers roun' heah," said Julius. "De fo'-foot ain' got no power. It has ter be de hin'-foot, suh,—de lef' hin'-foot er a grabe-ya'd rabbit, killt by a cross-eyed nigger on a da'k night in de full er de moon."

"They must be very rare and valuable," I said.

"Dey is kinder ska'ce, suh, en dey ain' no 'mount er money could buy mine, suh. I mought len' it ter anybody I sot sto' by, but I wouldn' sell it, no indeed, suh, I wouldn'."

"How do you know it brings good luck?" I asked.

"'Co'se I ain' had no bad luck sence I had it, suh, en I's had dis rabbit foot fer fo'ty yeahs. I had a good marster befo' de wah, en I wa'n't sol' erway, en I wuz sot free; en dat 'uz all good luck."

"But that doesn't prove anything," I rejoined. "Many other people have gone through a similar experience, and probably more than one of them had no rabbit's foot."

"Law, suh! you doan hafter prove 'bout de rabbit foot! Eve'ybody knows dat; leas'ways eve'ybody roun' heah knows it. But ef it has ter be prove' ter folks w'at wa'n't bawn en raise' in dis naberhood, dey is a' easy way ter prove it. Is I eber tol' you de tale er Sis' Becky en her pickaninny?"

"No," I said, "let us hear it." I thought perhaps the story might interest my wife as much or more than the novel I had meant to read from.

"Dis yer Becky," Julius began, "useter b'long ter ole Kunnel Pen'leton, who owned a plantation down on de Wim'l'ton Road, 'bout ten miles fum heah, des befo' you gits ter Black Swamp. Dis yer Becky wuz a fiel'-han', en a monst'us good 'un. She had a husban' oncet, a nigger w'at b'longed on de nex' plantation, but de man w'at owned her husban' died, en his lan' en his niggers had ter be sol' fer ter pay his debts. Kunnel Pen'leton 'lowed he'd 'a' bought dis nigger, but he had be'n bettin' on hoss races, en didn' hab no money, en so Becky's husban' wuz sol' erway ter Fuhginny.

"Co'se Becky went on some 'bout losin' her man, but she couldn' he'p herse'f; en 'sides dat, she had her pickaninny fer ter comfo't her. Dis yer little Mose wuz de cutes', blackes', shiny-eyedes' little nigger you eber laid eyes on, en he wuz ez fon' er his mammy ez his mammy wuz er him. Co'se Becky had ter wuk en didn' hab much time ter was'e wid her baby. Ole Aun' Nancy, de plantation nuss down at de qua'ters, useter take keer er little Mose in de daytime, en atter de niggers come in fum de cotton-fiel' Becky 'ud git her chile en kiss 'im en nuss 'im, en keep 'im 'tel mawnin'; en on Sundays she'd hab 'im in her cabin wid her all day long.

"Sis' Becky had got sorter useter gittin' 'long widout her husban', w'en one day Kunnel Pen'leton went ter de races. Co'se w'en he went ter de races, he tuk his hosses, en co'se he bet on 'is own hosses, en co'se he los' his money; fer Kunnel Pen'leton didn' nebber hab no luck wid his hosses, ef he did keep hisse'f po' projeckin' wid 'em. But dis time dey wuz a hoss name' Lightnin' Bug, w'at b'longed ter ernudder man, en dis hoss won de sweep-stakes; en Kunnel Pen'leton tuk a lackin' ter dat hoss, en ax' his owner w'at he wuz willin' ter take fer 'im.

"'I'll take a thousan' dollahs fer dat hoss,' sez dis yer man, who had a big plantation down to'd Wiun'l'ton, whar he raise' hosses fer ter race en ter sell.

"Well, Kunnel Pen'leton scratch' 'is head, en wonder whar he wuz gwine ter raise a thousan' dollahs; en he didn' see des how he could do it, fer he owed ez much ez he could borry a'ready on de skyo'ity he could gib. But he wuz des boun' ter hab dat hoss, so sezee:—

"'I'll gib you my note fer 'leven hund'ed dollahs fer dat hoss.'

"De yuther man shuck 'is head, en sezee:—

"'Yo' note, suh, is better 'n gol', I doan doubt; but I is made it a rule in my bizness not ter take no notes fum nobody. Howsomeber, suh, ef you is kinder sho't er fun's, mos' lackly we kin make some kin' er bahg'in. En w'iles we is talkin', I mought's well say dat I needs ernudder good nigger down on my place. Ef you is got a good one ter spar', I mought trade wid you.'

"Now, Kunnel Pen'leton didn' r'ally hab no niggers fer ter spar', but he 'lowed ter hisse'f he wuz des bleedzd ter hab dat hoss, en so he sez, sezee:—

"'Well, I doan lack ter, but I reckon I'll haf ter. You come out ter my plantation ter-morrer en look ober my niggers, en pick out de one you wants.'

"So sho' 'nuff nex' day dis yer man come out ter Kunnel Pen'leton's place en rid roun' de plantation en glanshed at de niggers, en who sh'd he pick out fum 'em all but Sis' Becky.

"'I needs a noo nigger 'oman down ter my place,' sezee, 'fer ter cook en wash, en so on; en dat young 'oman'll des fill de bill. You gimme her, en you kin hab Lightnin' Bug.'"

"Now, Kunnel Pen'leton didn' lack ter trade Sis' Becky, 'ca'se she wuz nigh 'bout de bes' fiel'-han' he had; en 'sides, he didn' keer ter take de mammies 'way fum dey chillun w'iles de chillun wuz little. But dis man say he want Becky, er e'se Kunnel Pen'leton couldn' hab de race hoss.

"'Well,' sez de kunnel, 'you kin hab de 'oman. But I doan lack ter sen' her 'way fum her baby. W'at'll you gimme fer dat nigger baby?'

"'I doan want de baby,' sez de yuther man. 'I ain' got no use fer de baby.'

"'I tell yer w'at I'll do,' 'lows Kunnel Pen'leton, 'I'll th'ow dat pick-aninny in fer good measure.'

"But de yuther man shuck his head. 'No,' sezee, 'I's much erbleedzd, but I doan raise niggers; I raises hosses, en I doan wanter be both'rin' wid no nigger babies. Nemmine de baby. I'll keep dat 'oman so busy she'll fergit de baby; fer niggers is made ter wuk, en dey ain' got no time fer no sich foolis'ness ez babies.'

"Kunnel Pen'leton didn' wanter hu't Becky's feelin's,—fer Kunnel Pen'leton wuz a kin'-hea'ted man, en nebber lack' ter make no trouble fer nobody,—en so he tol' Becky he wuz gwine sen' her down ter Robeson County fer a day er so, ter he'p out his son-in-law in his wuk; en bein' ez dis yuther man wuz gwine dat way, he had ax' 'im ter take her 'long in his buggy.

"'Kin I kyar little Mose wid me, marster?' ax' Sis' Becky.

"'N-o,' sez de kunnel, ez ef he wuz studyin' whuther ter let her take 'im er no; 'I reckon you better let Aun' Nancy look atter yo' baby fer de day er two you'll be gone, en she'll see dat he gits ernuff ter eat 'tel you gits back.'

"So Sis' Becky hug' en kiss' little Mose, en tol' 'im ter be a good lit-tle pickaninny, en take keer er hisse'f, en not fergit his mammy w'iles she wuz gone. En little Mose put his arms roun' his mammy en lafft en crowed des lack it wuz monst'us fine fun fer his mammy ter go 'way en leabe 'im.

"Well, dis yer hoss trader sta'ted out wid Becky, en bimeby, atter dey'd gone down de Lumbe'ton Road fer a few miles er so, dis man tu'nt roun' in a diffe'nt d'rection, en kep goin' dat erway, 'tel bimeby Sis' Becky up 'n ax' 'im ef he wuz gwine ter Robeson County by a noo road.

"'No, nigger,' sezee, 'I ain' gwine ter Robeson County at all. I's gwine ter Bladen County, whar my plantation is, en whar I raises all my hosses.'

"'But how is I gwine ter git ter Mis' Laura's plantation down in Robeson County?' sez Becky, wid her heart in her mouf, fer she 'mence' ter git skeered all er a sudden.

"'You ain' gwine ter git dere at all,' sez de man. 'You b'longs ter me now, fer I done traded my bes' race hoss fer you, wid yo' ole marster. Ef you is a good gal, I'll treat you right, en ef you doan behabe yo'se'f,— w'y, w'at e'se happens'll be yo' own fault.'

"Co'se Sis' Becky cried en went on 'bout her pickaninny, but co'se it didn' do no good, en bimeby dey got down ter dis yer man's place, en he put Sis' Becky ter wuk, en fergot all 'bout her habin' a pickaninny.

"Meanw'iles, w'en ebenin' come, de day Sis' Becky wuz tuk 'way, little Mose 'mence' ter git res'less, en bimeby, w'en his mammy didn' come, he sta'ted ter cry fer 'er. Aun' Nancy fed 'im en rocked 'im en rocked 'im, en fin'ly he des cried en cried 'tel he cried hisse'f ter sleep.

"De nex' day he didn' 'pear ter be as peart ez yushal, en w'en night come he fretted en went on wuss 'n he did de night befo'. De nex' day his little eyes 'mence' ter lose dey shine, en he wouldn' eat nuffin, en he 'mence' ter look so peaked dat Aun' Nancy tuk 'n kyared 'im up ter de big house, en showed 'im ter her ole missis, en her ole missis gin her some med'cinc fer 'im, en 'lowed ef he didn' git no better she sh'd fetch 'im up ter de big house ag'in, en dey'd hab a doctor, en nuss little Mose up dere. Fer Aun' Nancy's ole missis 'lowed he wuz a lackly little nigger en wu'th raisin'.

"But Aun' Nancy had l'arn' ter lack little Mose, en she didn' wan-ter hab 'im tuk up ter de big house. En so w'en he didn' git no better, she gethered a mess er green peas, an' tuk de peas en de baby, en went ter see ole Aun' Peggy, de cunjuh 'oman down by de Wim'l'ton Road. She gun Aun' Peggy de mess er peas, en tol' her all 'bout Sis' Becky en little Mose.

"'Dat is a monst'us small mess er peas you is fotch' me,' sez Aun' Peggy, sez she.

"'Yas, I knows,' 'lowed Aun' Nancy, 'but dis yere is a monst'us small pickaninny.'

"'You'll hafter fetch me sump'n mo',' sez Aun' Peggy, 'fer you can't 'spec' me ter was'e my time diggin' roots en wukkin' cunj'ation fer nuffin.'

"'All right,' sez Aun' Nancy, 'I'll fetch you sump'n mo' nex' time.'

"'You bettah,' sez Aun' Peggy, 'er e'se dey'll be trouble. W'at dis yer little pickaninny needs is ter see his mammy. You leabe 'im heah 'tel ebenin' en I'll show 'im his mammy.'

"So w'en Aun' Nancy had gone 'way, Aun' Peggy tuk 'n wukked her roots, en tu'nt little Mose ter a hummin'-bird, en sont 'im off fer ter fin' his mammy.

"So little Mose flewed, en flewed, en flewed away, 'tel bimeby he got ter de place whar Sis' Becky b'longed. He seed his mammy wukkin' roun' de ya'd, en he could tell fum lookin' at her dat she wuz trouble' in her min' 'bout sump'n, en feelin' kin' er po'ly. Sis' Becky heared sump'n hummin' roun' en roun' her, sweet en low. Fus' she 'lowed it wuz a hummin'-bird; den she thought it sounded lack her little Mose croonin' on her breas' way back yander on de ole plantation. En she des 'magine' it wuz her little Mose, en it made her feel bettah, en she went on 'bout her wuk pearter 'n she'd done sence she'd be'n down dere. Little Mose stayed roun' 'tel late in de ebenin', en den flewed back ez hard ez he could ter Aun' Peggy. Ez fer Sis' Becky, she dremp all dat night dat she wuz holdin' her pickaninny in her arms, en kissin' him, en nussin' him, des lack she useter do back on de old plantation whar he wuz bawn. En fer th'ee er fo' days Sis' Becky went 'bout her wuk wid mo' sperrit dan she'd showed sence she'd be'n down dere ter dis man's plantation.

"De nex' day atter he come back, little Mose wuz mo' pearter en better 'n he had be'n fer a long time. But to'ds de een' er de week he 'mence' ter git res'less ag'in, en stop' eatin', en Aun' Nancy kyared 'im down ter Aun' Peggy once mo', en she tu'nt 'im ter a mawkin'-bird dis time, en sont 'im off ter see his mammy ag'in.

"It didn' take him long fer ter git dere, en w'en he did, he seed his mammy standin' in de kitchen, lookin' back in de d'rection little Mose wuz comin' fum. En dey wuz tears in her eyes, en she look' mo' po'ly en peaked 'n she had w'en he wuz down dere befo'. So little Mose sot on a tree in de ya'd en sung, en sung, en sung, des fittin' ter split his th'oat. Fus' Sis' Becky didn' notice 'im much, but dis mawkin'-bird kep' stayin' roun' de house all day, en bimeby Sis' Becky des 'magine' dat mawkin'-bird wuz her little Mose crowin' en crowin', des lack he useter do w'en his mammy would come home at night fum de cotton-fiel'. De mawkin'-bird stayed roun' dere 'mos' all day, en w'en Sis' Becky went out in de ya'd one time, dis yer mawkin'-bird lit on her shoulder en peck' at de piece er bread she wuz eatin', en fluttered his wings so dey rub' up agin de side er her head. En w'en he flewed away 'long late in de ebenin', des 'fo' sundown, Sis' Becky felt mo' better 'n she had sence she had heared dat hummin'-bird a week er so pas'. En dat night she dremp 'bout ole times ag'in, des lack she did befo'.

"But dis yer totin' little Mose down ter ole Aun' Peggy, en dis yer gittin' things fer ter pay de cunjuh 'oman, use' up a lot er Aun' Nancy's time, en she begun ter git kinder ti'ed. 'Sides dat, w'en Sis' Becky had be'n on de plantation, she had useter he'p Aun' Nancy wid de young uns ebenin's en Sundays; en Aun' Nancy 'mence' ter miss 'er monst'us, 'speshly sence she got a tech er de rheumatiz herse'f, en so she 'lows ter ole Aun' Peggy one day:—

"'Aun' Peggy, ain' dey no way you kin fetch Sis' Becky back home?'

"'Huh!' sez Aun' Peggy, 'I dunno 'bout dat. I'll hafter wuk my roots en fin' out whuther I kin er no. But it'll take a monst'us heap er wuk, en I can't was'e my time fer nuffin. Ef you'll fetch me sump'n ter pay me fer my trouble, I reckon we kin fix it.'

"So nex' day Aun' Nancy went down ter see Aun' Peggy ag'in.

"'Aun' Peggy,' sez she, 'I is fotch' you my bes' Sunday head-han-kercher. Will dat do?'

"Aun' Peggy look' at de head-hankercher, en run her han' ober it, en sez she:—

"'Yas, dat'll do fus'-rate. I's be'n wukkin' my roots sence you be'n gone, en I 'lows mos' lackly I kin git Sis' Becky back, but it's gwine take fig'rin' en studyin' ez well ez cunj'in'. De fus' thing ter do'll be ter stop fetchin' dat pickaninny down heah, en not sen' 'im ter see his mammy no mo'. Ef he gits too po'ly, you lemme know, en I'll gib you some kin' er mixtry fer ter make 'im fergit Sis' Becky fer a week er so. So 'less'n you comes fer dat, you neenter come back ter see me no mo' 'tel I sen's fer you.'

"So Aun' Peggy sont Aun' Nancy erway, en de fus' thing she done wuz ter call a hawnet fum a nes' unner her eaves.

"'You go up ter Kunnel Pen'leton's stable, hawnet,' sez she, 'en sting de knees er de race hoss name' Lightnin' Bug. Bc sho' en git de right one.'

"So de hawnet flewed up ter Kunnel Pen'leton's stable en stung Lightnin' Bug roun' de laigs, en de nex' mawnin' Lightnin' Bug's knees wuz all swoll' up, twice't ez big ez dey oughter be. W'en Kunnel Pen'leton went out ter de stable en see de hoss's laigs, hit would 'a' des made you trimble lack a leaf fer ter heah him cuss dat hoss trader. Howsomeber, he cool' off bimeby en tol' de stable boy fer ter rub Lightnin' Bug's laigs wid some linimum. De boy done ez his marster tol' 'im, en by de nex' day de swellin' had gone down consid'able. Aun' Peggy had sont a sparrer, w'at had a nes' in one er de trees close ter her cabin, fer ter watch w'at wuz gwine on 'roun' de big house, en w'en dis yer sparrer tol' 'er de hoss wuz gittin' ober de swellin', she sont de hawnet back fer ter sting 'is knees some mo', en de nex' mawnin' Lightnin' Bug's laigs wuz swoll' up wuss 'n befo'.

"Well, dis time Kunnel Pen'leton wuz mad th'oo en th'oo, en all de way 'roun', en he cusst dat hoss trader up en down, fum A ter *Izzard*. He cusst so ha'd dat de stable boy got 'mos' skeered ter def, en went off en hid hisse'f in de hay.

"Ez fer Kunnel Pen'leton, he went right up ter de house en got out his pen en ink, en tuk off his coat en roll' up his sleeves, en writ a letter ter dis hoss trader, en sezee: —

"'You is sol' me a hoss w'at is got a ringbone er a spavin er sump'n, en w'at I paid you fer wuz a soun' hoss. I wants you ter sen' my nigger 'oman back en take yo' ole hoss, er e'se I'll sue you, sho's you bawn.'

"But dis yer man wa'n't skeered a bit, en he writ back ter Kunnel Pen'leton dat a bahg'in wuz a bahg'in; dat Lightnin' Bug wuz soun' w'en he sol' 'im, en ef Kunnel Pen'leton didn' knowed ernuff 'bout hosses ter take keer er a fine racer, dat wuz his own fune'al. En he say Kunnel Pen'leton kin sue en be cusst fer all he keer, but he ain' gwine ter gib up de nigger he bought en paid fer.

"W'en Kunnel Pen'leton got dis letter he wuz madder 'n he wuz befo', 'speshly 'ca'se dis man 'lowed he didn' know how ter take keer er fine hosses. But he couldn' do nuffin but fotch a lawsuit, en he knowed, by his own 'spe'ience, dat lawsuits wuz slow ez de seben-yeah eetch and cos' mo' d'n dey come ter, en he 'lowed he better go slow en wait awhile.

"Aun' Peggy knowed w'at wuz gwine on all dis time, en she fix' up a little bag wid some roots en one thing en ernudder in it, en gun it ter dis sparrer er her'n, en tol' 'im ter take it 'way down yander whar Sis' Becky wuz, en drap it right befo' de do' er her cabin, so she'd be sho' en fin' it de fus' time she come out'n de do'.

"One night Sis' Becky dremp' her pickaninny wuz dead, en de nex' day she wuz mo'nin' en groanin' all day. She dremp' de same dream th'ee nights runnin', en den, de nex' mawnin' atter de las' night, she foun' dis yer little bag de sparrer had drap' in front her do'; en she 'lowed she'd be'n cunju'd, en wuz gwine ter die, en ez long ez her pickaninny wuz dead dey wa'n't no use tryin' ter do nuffin nohow. En so she tuk 'n' went ter bed, en tol' her marster she'd be'n cunju'd en wuz gwine ter die.

"Her marster lafft at her, en argyed wid her, en tried ter 'suade her out'n dis yer fool notion, ez he called it, — fer he wuz one er dese yer w'ite folks w'at purten' dey doan b'liebe in cunj'in', — but hit wa'n't no use. Sis' Becky kep' gittin' wusser en wusser, 'tel fin'ly dis yer man 'lowed Sis' Becky wuz gwine ter die, sho' 'nuff. En ez he knowed dey hadn' be'n nuffin de matter wid Lightnin' Bug w'en he traded 'im, he 'lowed mebbe he could kyo' 'im en fetch 'im roun' all right, leas'ways good 'nuff ter sell ag'in. En anyhow, a lame hoss wuz better 'n a dead nigger. So he sot down en writ Kunnel Pen'leton a letter.

"'My conscience,' sezee, 'has be'n troublin' me 'bout dat ringbone' hoss I sol' you. Some folks 'lows a hoss trader ain' got no conscience, but dey doan know me, fer dat is my weak spot, en de reason I ain' made no mo' money hoss tradin'. Fac' is,' sezee, 'I is got so I can't sleep nights fum studyin' 'bout dat spavin' hoss; en I is made up my min' dat, w'iles a bahg'in is a bahg'in, en you seed Lightnin' Bug befo' you traded fer 'im, principle is wuth mo' d'n money er hosses er niggers. So ef you'll sen' Lightnin' Bug down heah, I'll sen' yo' nigger 'oman back, en we'll call de trade off, en be ez good frien's ez we eber wuz, en no ha'd feelin's.'

"So sho' 'nuff, Kunnel Pen'leton sont de hoss back. En w'en de man w'at come ter bring Lightnin' Bug tol' Sis' Becky her pickaninny wa'n't dead, Sis' Becky wuz so glad dat she 'lowed she wuz gwine ter try ter lib 'tel she got back whar she could see little Mose once mo'. En w'en she retch' de ole plantation en seed her baby kickin' en crowin' en holdin' out his little arms to'd her, she wush' she wuzn' conju'd en didn' hafter die. En w'en Aun' Nancy tol' 'er all 'bout Aun' Peggy, Sis' Becky went down ter see de cunjuh 'oman, en Aun' Peggy tol' her she had cunju'd her. En den Aun' Peggy tuk de goopher off'n her, en she got well, en stayed on de plantation, en raise' her pickaninny. En w'en little Mose growed up, he could sing en whistle des lack a mawkin'-bird, so dat de w'ite folks useter hab 'im come up ter de big house at night, en whistle en sing fer 'em, en dey useter gib 'im money en vit-tles en one thing er ernudder, w'ich he alluz tuk home ter his mammy; fer he knowed all 'bout w'at she had gone th'oo. He tu'nt out ter be a sma't man, en l'arnt de blacksmif trade; en Kunnel Pen'leton let 'im hire his time. En bimeby he bought his mammy en sot her free, en den he bought hisse'f, en tuk keer er Sis' Becky ez long ez dey bofe libbed."

My wife had listened to this story with greater interest than she had manifested in any subject for several days. I had watched her furtively from time to time during the recital, and had observed the play of her countenance. It had expressed in turn sympathy, indignation, pity, and at the end lively satisfaction.

"That is a very ingenious fairy tale, Julius," I said, "and we are much obliged to you."

"Why, John!" said my wife severely, "the story bears the stamp of truth, if ever a story did."

"Yes," I replied, "especially the humming-bird episode, and the mocking-bird digression, to say nothing of the doings of the hornet and the sparrow."

"Oh, well, I don't care," she rejoined, with delightful animation; "those are mere ornamental details and not at all essential. The story is true to nature, and might have happened half a hundred times, and no doubt did happen, in those horrid days before the war."

"By the way, Julius," I remarked, "your story doesn't establish what you started out to prove,—that a rabbit's foot brings good luck."

"Hit's plain 'nuff ter me, suh," replied Julius. "I bet young missis dere kin 'splain it herse'f."

"I rather suspect," replied my wife promptly, "that Sis' Becky had no rabbit's foot."

"You is hit de bull's-eye de fus' fire, ma'm," assented Julius. "Ef Sis' Becky had had a rabbit foot, she nebber would 'a' went th'oo all dis trouble."

I went into the house for some purpose, and left Julius talking to my wife. When I came back a moment later, he was gone.

My wife's condition took a turn for the better from this very day, and she was soon on the way to ultimate recovery. Several weeks later, after she had resumed her afternoon drives, which had been interrupted by her illness, Julius brought the rockaway round to the front door one day, and I assisted my wife into the carriage.

"John," she said, before I had taken my seat, "I wish you would look in my room, and bring me my handkerchief. You will find it in the pocket of my blue dress."

I went to execute the commission. When I pulled the handkerchief out of her pocket, something else came with it and fell on the floor. I picked up the object and looked at it. It was Julius's rabbit's foot.

A MATTER OF PRINCIPLE

I

"WHAT OUR country needs most in its treatment of the race problem," observed Mr. Cicero Clayton at one of the monthly meetings of the Blue Vein Society, of which he was a prominent member, "is a clearer conception of the brotherhood of man."

The same sentiment in much the same words had often fallen from Mr. Clayton's lips,—so often, in fact, that the younger members of the society sometimes spoke of him—among themselves of course—as "Brotherhood Clayton." The sobriquet derived its point from the application he made of the principle involved in this oft-repeated proposition.

The fundamental article of Mr. Clayton's social creed was that he himself was not a negro.

"I know," he would say, "that the white people lump us all together as negroes, and condemn us all to the same social ostracism. But I don't accept this classification, for my part, and I imagine that, as the chief party in interest, I have a right to my opinion. People who belong by half or more of their blood to the most virile and progressive race of modern times have as much right to call themselves white as others have to call them negroes."

Mr. Clayton spoke warmly, for he was well informed, and had thought much upon the subject; too much, indeed, for he had not been able to escape entirely the tendency of too much concentration upon one subject to make even the clearest minds morbid.

"Of course we can't enforce our claims, or protect ourselves from being robbed of our birthright; but we can at least have principles, and try to live up to them the best we can. If we are not accepted as white, we can at any rate make it clear that we object to being called black. Our protest cannot fail in time to impress itself upon the better class of

67

white people; for the Anglo-Saxon race loves justice, and will eventually do it, where it does not conflict with their own interests."

Whether or not the fact that Mr. Clayton meant no sarcasm, and was conscious of no inconsistency in this eulogy, tended to establish the racial identity he claimed may safely be left to the discerning reader.

In living up to his creed Mr. Clayton declined to associate to any considerable extent with black people. This was sometimes a little inconvenient, and occasionally involved a sacrifice of some pleasure for himself and his family, because they would not attend entertainments where many black people were likely to be present. But they had a social refuge in a little society of people like themselves; they attended, too, a church, of which nearly all the members were white, and they were connected with a number of the religious and benevolent associations open to all good citizens, where they came into contact with the better class of white people, and were treated, in their capacity of members, with a courtesy and consideration scarcely different from that accorded to other citizens.

Mr. Clayton's racial theory was not only logical enough, but was in his own case backed up by substantial arguments. He had begun life with a small patrimony, and had invested his money in a restaurant, which by careful and judicious attention had grown from a cheap eating-house into the most popular and successful confectionery and catering establishment in Groveland. His business occupied a double store on Oakwood Avenue. He owned houses and lots, and stocks and bonds, had good credit at the banks, and lived in a style befitting his income and business standing. In person he was of olive complexion, with slightly curly hair. His features approached the Cuban or Latin-American type rather than the familiar broad characteristics of the mulatto, this suggestion of something foreign being heightened by a Vandyke beard and a carefully waxed and pointed mustache. When he walked to church on Sunday mornings with his daughter Alice, they were a couple of such striking appearance as surely to attract attention.

Miss Alice Clayton was queen of her social set. She was young, she was handsome. She was nearly white; she frankly confessed her sorrow that she was not entirely so. She was accomplished and amiable, dressed in good taste, and had for her father by all odds the richest colored man—the term is used with apologies to Mr. Clayton, explaining that it does not necessarily mean a negro—in Groveland. So pronounced was her superiority that really she had but one social rival worthy of the name,—Miss Lura Watkins, whose father kept a prosperous livery stable and lived in almost as good style as the Claytons. Miss Watkins, while good-looking enough, was not so young nor quite so white as Miss Clayton. She was popular, however, among their mutual acquaintances, and there was a good-natured race between the two as to which should make the first and best marriage.

Marriages among Miss Clayton's set were serious affairs. Of course marriage is always a serious matter, whether it be a success or a failure, and there are those who believe that any marriage is better than no marriage. But among Miss Clayton's friends and associates matrimony took on an added seriousness because of the very narrow limits within which it could take place. Miss Clayton and her friends, by reason of their assumed superiority to black people, or perhaps as much by reason of a somewhat morbid shrinking from the curiosity manifested toward married people of strongly contrasting colors, would not marry black men, and except in rare instances white men would not marry them. They were therefore restricted for a choice to the young men of their own complexion. But these, unfortunately for the girls, had a wider choice. In any State where the laws permit freedom of the marriage contract, a man, by virtue of his sex, can find a wife of whatever complexion he prefers; of course he must not always ask too much in other respects, for most women like to better their social position when they marry. To the number thus lost by "going on the other side," as the phrase went, add the worthless contingent whom no self-respecting woman would marry, and the choice was still further restricted; so that it had become fashionable, when the supply of eligible men ran short, for those of Miss Clayton's set who could afford it to go traveling, ostensibly for pleasure, but with the serious hope that they might meet their fate away from home.

Miss Clayton had perhaps a larger option than any of her associates. Among such men as there were she could have taken her choice. Her beauty, her position, her accomplishments, her father's wealth, all made her eminently desirable. But, on the other hand, the same things rendered her more difficult to reach, and harder to please. To get access to her heart, too, it was necessary to run the gauntlet of her parents, which, until she had reached the age of twenty-three, no one had succeeded in doing safely. Many had called, but none had been chosen.

There was, however, one spot left unguarded, and through it Cupid, a veteran sharpshooter, sent a dart. Mr. Clayton had taken into his service and into his household a poor relation, a sort of cousin several times removed. This boy—his name was Jack—had gone into Mr. Clayton's service at a very youthful age,—twelve or thirteen. He had helped about the housework, washed the dishes, swept the floors, taken care of the lawn and the stable for three or four years, while he attended school. His cousin had then taken him into the store, where he had swept the floor, washed the windows, and done a class of work that kept fully impressed upon him the fact that he was a poor dependent.

Nevertheless he was a cheerful lad, who took what he could get and was properly grateful, but always meant to get more. By sheer force of industry and affability and shrewdness, he forced his employer to promote him in time to a position of recognized authority in the establishment. Any one outside of the family would have perceived in him a very suitable husband for Miss Clayton; he was of about the same age, or a year or two older, was as fair of complexion as she, when she was not powdered, and was passably good-looking, with a bearing of which the natural manliness had been no more warped than his training and racial status had rendered inevitable; for he had early learned the law of growth, that to bend is better than to break. He was sometimes sent to accompany Miss Clayton to places in the evening, when she had no other escort, and it is quite likely that she discovered his good points before her parents did. That they should in time perceive them was inevitable. But even then, so accustomed were they to looking down upon the object of their former bounty, that they only spoke of the matter jocularly.

"Well, Alice," her father would say in his bluff way, "you'll not be absolutely obliged to die an old maid. If we can't find anything better for you, there's always Jack. As long as he doesn't take to some other girl, you can fall back on him as a last chance. He'd be glad to take you to get into the business."

Miss Alice had considered the joke a very poor one when first made, but by occasional repetition she became somewhat familiar with it. In time it got around to Jack himself, to whom it seemed no joke at all. He had long considered it a consummation devoutly to be wished, and when he became aware that the possibility of such a match had occurred to the other parties in interest, he made up his mind that the idea should in due course of time become an accomplished fact. He had even suggested as much to Alice, in a casual way, to feel his ground; and while she had treated the matter lightly, he was not without hope that she had been impressed by the suggestion. Before he had had time, however, to follow up this lead, Miss Clayton, in the spring of 187–, went away on a visit to Washington.

The occasion of her visit was a presidential inauguration. The new President owed his nomination mainly to the votes of the Southern delegates in the convention, and was believed to be correspondingly well disposed to the race from which the Southern delegates were for the most part recruited. Friends of rival and unsuccessful candidates for the nomination had more than hinted that the Southern delegates were very substantially rewarded for their support at the time when it was given; whether this was true or not the parties concerned know best. At any rate the colored politicians did not see it in that light, for they were gathered from near and far to press their claims for recognition and patronage. On the evening following the White House inaugural ball, the colored people of Washington gave an "inaugural" ball at a large public hall. It was under the management of their leading citizens, among them several high officials holding over from the last administration, and a number of professional and business men. This ball was the most noteworthy social event that colored circles up to that time had ever known. There were many visitors from various parts of the country. Miss Clayton attended the ball, the honors of which she carried away easily. She danced with several partners, and was introduced to innumerable people whom she had never seen before, and whom she hardly expected ever to meet again. She went away from the ball, at four o'clock in the morning, in a glow of triumph, and with a confused impression of senators and representatives and lawyers and doctors of all shades, who had sought an introduction, led her through the dance, and overwhelmed her with compliments. She returned home the next day but one, after the most delightful week of her life.

II

One afternoon, about three weeks after her return from Washington, Alice received a letter through the mail. The envelope bore the words "House of Representatives" printed in one corner, and in the opposite corner, in a bold running hand, a Congressmen's frank, "Hamilton M. Brown, M. C." The letter read as follows:—

HOUSE OF REPRESENTATIVES,
WASHINGTON, D. C., March 30, 187–.

MISS ALICE CLAYTON, GROVELAND.

DEAR FRIEND (if I may be permitted to call you so after so brief an acquaintance),—I remember with sincerest pleasure our recent meeting at the inaugural ball, and the sensation created by your beauty, your amiable manners, and your graceful dancing. Time has so strengthened the impression I then received, that I should have felt inconsolable had I thought it impossible ever to again behold the charms which had brightened the occasion of our meeting and eclipsed by their brilliancy the leading belles of the capital. I had hoped, however, to have the pleasure of meeting you again, and circumstances have fortunately placed it in my power to do so at an early date. You have doubtless learned that the contest over the election in the Sixth Congressional District of South Carolina has been decided in my favor, and that I now have the honor of representing my native State at the national capital.

I have just been appointed a member of a special committee to visit and inspect the Sault River and the Straits of Mackinac, with reference to the needs of lake navigation. I have made arrangements to start a week ahead of the other members of the committee, whom I am to meet in Detroit on the 20th. I shall leave here on the 2d, and will arrive in Groveland on the 3d, by the 7.30 evening express. I shall remain in Groveland several days, in the course of which I shall be pleased to call, and renew the acquaintance so auspiciously begun in Washington, which it is my fondest hope may ripen into a warmer friendship.

If you do not regard my visit as presumptuous, and do not write me in the mean while forbidding it, I shall do myself the pleasure of waiting on you the morning after my arrival in Groveland.

With renewed expressions of my sincere admiration and profound esteem, I remain,

Sincerely yours,
HAMILTON M. BROWN, M. C.

To Alice, and especially to her mother, this bold and flowery letter had very nearly the force of a formal declaration. They read it over again and again, and spent most of the afternoon discussing it. There were few young men in Groveland eligible as husbands for so superior a person as Alice Clayton, and an addition to the number would be very acceptable. but the mere fact of his being a Congressman was not sufficient to qualify him; there were other considerations.

"I've never heard of this Honorable Hamilton M. Brown," said Mr. Clayton. The letter had been laid before him at the supper-table. "It's strange, Alice, that you haven't said anything about him before. You must have met lots of swell folks not to recollect a Congressman."

"But he wasn't a Congressman then," answered Alice; "he was only a claimant. I remember Senator Bruce, and Mr. Douglass; but there were so many doctors and lawyers and politicians that I couldn't keep track of them all. Still I have a faint impression of a Mr. Brown who danced with me."

She went into the parlor and brought out the dancing programme she had used at the Washington ball. She had decorated it with a bow of blue ribbon and preserved it as a souvenir of her visit.

"Yes," she said, after examining it, "I must have danced with him. Here are the initials—'H. M. B.'"

"What color is he," asked Mr. Clayton, as he plied his knife and fork. "I have a notion that he was rather dark—darker than any one I had ever danced with before."

"Why did you dance with him?" asked her father. "You weren't obliged to go back on your principles because you were away from home."

"Well, father, 'when you're in Rome'—you know the rest. Mrs. Clearweather introduced me to several dark men, to him among others. They were her friends, and common decency required me to be courteous."

"If this man is black, we don't want to encourage him. If he's the right sort, we'll invite him to the house."

"And make him feel at home," added Mrs. Clayton, on hospitable thoughts intent.

"We must ask Sadler about him to-morrow," said Mr. Clayton, when he had drunk his coffee and lighted his cigar. "If he's the right man he shall have cause to remember his visit to Groveland. We'll show him that Washington is not the only town on earth."

The uncertainty of the family with regard to Mr. Brown was soon removed. Mr. Solomon Sadler, who was supposed to know everything worth knowing concerning the colored race, and everybody of importance connected with it, dropped in after supper to make an evening call. Sadler was familiar with the history of every man of negro ancestry who had distinguished himself in any walk of life. He could give the pedigree of Alexander Pushkin, the titles of scores of Dumas's novels (even Sadler had not time to learn them all), and could recite the whole of Wendell Phillips's lecture on Toussaint l'Ouverture. He claimed a personal acquaintance with Mr. Frederick Douglass, and had been often in Washington, where he was well known and well received in good colored society.

"Let me see," he said reflectively, when asked for information about the Honorable Hamilton M. Brown. "Yes, I think I know him. He studied at Oberlin just after the war. He was about leaving there when I entered. There were two H. M. Browns there—a Hamilton M. Brown and a Henry M. Brown. One was stout and dark and the other was slim and quite light; you could scarcely tell him from a dark white man. They used to call them 'light Brown' and 'dark Brown.' I didn't know either of them except by sight, for they were there only a few weeks after I went in. As I remember them, Hamilton was the fair one—a very good-looking, gentlemanly fellow, and, as I heard, a good student and a fine speaker."

"Do you remember what kind of hair he had?" asked Mr. Clayton.

"Very good indeed; straight, as I remember it. He looked something like a Spaniard or a Portuguese."

"Now that you describe him," said Alice, "I remember quite well dancing with such a gentleman; and I'm wrong about my 'H. M. B.' The dark man must have been some one else; there are two others on my card that I can't remember distinctly, and he was probably one of those."

"I guess he's all right, Alice," said her father when Sadler had gone away. "He evidently means business, and we must treat him white. Of course he must stay with us; there are no hotels in Groveland while he is here. Let's see—he'll be here in three days. That isn't very long, but I guess we can get ready. I'll write a letter this afternoon—or you write it, and invite him to the house, and say I'll meet him at the depot. And you may have *carte blanche* for making the preparations."

"We must have some people to meet him."

"Certainly; a reception is the proper thing. Sit down immediately and write the letter and I'll mail it first thing in the morning, so he'll get it before he has time to make other arrangements. And you and your mother put your heads together and make out a list of guests, and I'll have the invitations printed to-morrow. We will show the darkeys of Groveland how to entertain a Congressman."

It will be noted that in moments of abstraction or excitement Mr. Clayton sometimes relapsed into forms of speech not entirely consistent with his principles. But some allowance must be made for his atmosphere; he could no more escape from it than the leopard can change his spots, or the— In deference to Mr. Clayton's feelings the quotation will be left incomplete.

Alice wrote the letter on the spot and it was duly mailed, and sped on its winged way to Washington.

The preparations for the reception were made as thoroughly and elaborately as possible on so short a notice. The invitations were issued; the house was cleaned from attic to cellar; an orchestra was engaged for the evening; elaborate floral decorations were planned and the flowers ordered. Even the refreshments, which ordinarily, in the household of a caterer, would be a mere matter of familiar detail, became a subject of serious consultation and study.

The approaching event was a matter of very much interest to the fortunate ones who were honored with invitations, and this for several reasons. They were anxious to meet this sole representative of their race in the —th Congress, and as he was not one of the old-line colored leaders, but a new star risen on the political horizon, there was a special curiosity to see who he was and what he looked like. Moreover, the Claytons did not often entertain a large company, but when they did, it was on a scale commensurate with their means and position, and to be present on such an occasion was a thing to remember and to talk about. And, most important consideration of all, some remarks dropped by members of the Clayton family had given rise to the rumor that the Congressman was seeking a wife. This invested his visit with a romantic interest, and gave the reception a practical value; for there were other marriageable girls besides Miss Clayton, and if one was left another might be taken.

III

On the evening of April 3d, at fifteen minutes of six o'clock, Mr. Clayton, accompanied by Jack, entered the livery carriage waiting at his gate and ordered the coachman to drive to the Union Depot. He had taken Jack along, partly for company, and partly that Jack might relieve the Congressman of any trouble about his baggage, and make himself useful in case of emergency. Jack was willing enough to go, for he had foreseen in the visitor a rival for Alice's hand,—indeed he had heard more or less of the subject for several days,—and was glad to make a reconnaissance before the enemy arrived upon the field of battle. He had made—at least he had thought so—considerable progress with Alice during the three weeks since her return from Washington, and once or twice Alice had been perilously near the tender stage. This visit had disturbed the situation and threatened to ruin his chances; but he did not mean to give up without a struggle.

Arrived at the main entrance, Mr. Clayton directed the carriage to wait, and entered the station with Jack. The Union Depot at Groveland was an immense oblong structure, covering a dozen parallel tracks and furnishing terminal passenger facilities for half a dozen railroads. The tracks ran east and west, and the depot was entered from the south, at about the middle of the building. On either side of the entrance, the waiting-rooms, refreshment rooms, baggage and express departments, and other administrative offices, extended in a row for the entire length of the building; and beyond them and parallel with them stretched a long open space, separated from the tracks by an iron fence or *grille*. There were two entrance gates in the fence, at which tickets must be shown before access could be had to trains, and two other gates, by which arriving passengers came out.

Mr. Clayton looked at the blackboard on the wall underneath the station clock, and observed that the 7.30 train from Washington was five minutes late. Accompanied by Jack, he walked up and down the platform until the train, with the usual accompaniment of panting steam and clanging bell and rumbling trucks, pulled into the station, and drew up on the third or fourth track from the iron railing. Mr. Clayton stationed himself at the gate nearest the rear end of the train, reasoning that the Congressman would ride in a parlor car, and would naturally come out by the gate nearest the point at which he left the train.

"You'd better go and stand by the other gate, Jack," he said to his companion, "and stop him if he goes out that way."

The train was well filled and a stream of passengers poured through. Mr. Clayton scanned the crowd carefully as they approached the gate, and scrutinized each passenger as he came through, without seeing any one that met the description of Congressman Brown, as given by Sadler, or any one that could in his opinion be the gentleman for whom he was looking. When the last one had passed through he was left to the conclusion that his expected guest had gone out by the other gate. Mr. Clayton hastened thither.

"Didn't he come out this way, Jack?" he asked.

"No, sir," replied the young man, "I haven't seen him."

"That's strange," mused Mr. Clayton, somewhat anxiously. "He would hardly fail to come without giving us notice. Surely we must have missed him. We'd better look around a little. You go that way and I'll go this."

Mr. Clayton turned and walked several rods along the platform to the men's waiting-room, and standing near the door glanced around to see if he could find the object of his search. The only colored person in the room was a stout and very black man, wearing a broadcloth suit and a silk hat, and seated a short distance from the door. On the seat by his side stood a couple of valises. On one of them, the one nearest him, on which his arm rested, was written, in white letters, plainly legible,—

H. M. BROWN, M. C.
Washington, D. C.

Mr. Clayton's feelings at this discovery can better be imagined than described. He hastily left the waiting-room, before the black gentleman, who was looking the other way, was even aware of his presence, and, walking rapidly up and down the platform, communed with himself upon what course of action the situation demanded. He had invited to his house, had come down to meet, had made elaborate preparations to entertain on the following evening, a light-colored man,—a white man by his theory, an acceptable guest, a possible husband for his daughter, an avowed suitor for her hand. If the Congressman had turned out to be brown, even dark brown, with fairly good hair, though he might not have desired him as a son-in-law, yet he could have welcomed him as a guest. But even this softening of the blow was denied him, for the man in the waiting-room was palpably, aggressively black, with pronounced African features and woolly hair, without apparently a single drop of redeeming white blood. Could he, in the face of his well-known principles, his lifelong rule of conduct, take this negro into his home and introduce him to his friends? Could he subject his wife and daughter to the rude shock of such a disappointment? It would be bad enough for them to learn of the ghastly mistake, but to have him in the house would be twisting the arrow in the wound.

Mr. Clayton had the instincts of a gentleman, and realized the delicacy of the situation. But to get out of this difficulty without wounding the feelings of the Congressman required not only diplomacy but dispatch. Whatever he did must be done promptly; for if he waited many minutes the Congressman would probably take a carriage and be driven to Mr. Clayton's residence.

A ray of hope came for a moment to illumine the gloom of the situation. Perhaps the black man was merely sitting there, and not the owner of the valise! For there were two valises, one on each side of the supposed Congressman. For obvious reasons he did not care to make the inquiry himself, so he looked around for his companion, who came up a moment later.

"Jack," he exclaimed excitedly, "I'm afraid we're in the worst kind of a hole, unless there's some mistake! Run down to the men's waiting-room and you'll see a man and a valise, and you'll understand what I mean. Ask that darkey if he is the Honorable Mr. Brown, Congressman from South Carolina. If he says yes, come back right away and let me know, without giving him time to ask any questions, and put your wits to work to help me out of the scrape."

"I wonder what's the matter?" said Jack to himself, but did as he was told. In a moment he came running back.

"Yes, sir," he announced; "he says he's the man."

"Jack," said Mr. Clayton desperately, "if you want to show your appreciation of what I've done for you, you must suggest some way out of this. I'd never dare to take that negro to my house, and yet I'm obliged to treat him like a gentleman."

Jack's eyes had worn a somewhat reflective look since he had gone to make the inquiry. Suddenly his face brightened with intelligence, and then, as a newsboy ran into the station calling his wares, hardened into determination.

"Clarion, special extry 'dition! All about de epidemic er dipt'eria!" clamored the newsboy with shrill childish treble, as he made his way toward the waiting-room. Jack darted after him, and saw the man to whom he had spoken buy a paper. He ran back to his employer, and dragged him over toward the ticket-seller's window.

"I have it, sir!" he exclaimed, seizing a telegraph blank and writing rapidly, and reading aloud as he wrote. "How's this for a way out?"—

"DEAR SIR,—I write you this note here in the depot to inform you of an unfortunate event which has interfered with my plans and those of my family for your entertainment while in Groveland.

Yesterday my daughter Alice complained of a sore throat, which by this afternoon had developed into a case of malignant diphtheria. In consequence our house has been quarantined; and while I have felt myself obliged to come down to the depot, I do not feel that I ought to expose you to the possibility of infection, and I therefore send you this by another hand. The bearer will conduct you to a carriage which I have ordered placed at your service, and unless you should prefer some other hotel, you will be driven to the Forest Hill House, where I beg you will consider yourself my guest during your stay in the city, and make the fullest use of every convenience it may offer. From present indications I fear no one of our family will be able to see you, which we shall regret beyond expression, as we have made elaborate arrangements for your entertainment. I still hope, however, that you may enjoy your visit, as there are many places of interest in the city, and many friends will doubtless be glad to make your acquaintance.

"With assurances of my profound regret, I am
Sincerely yours,
"Cicero Clayton."

"Splendid!" cried Mr. Clayton. "You've helped me out of a horrible scrape. Now, go and take him to the hotel and see him comfortably located, and tell them to charge the bill to me."

"I suspect, sir," suggested Jack, "that I'd better not go up to the house, and you'll have to stay in yourself a day or two, to keep up appearances. I'll sleep on the lounge at the store, and we can talk business over the telephone."

"All right, Jack, we'll arrange the details later. But for Heaven's sake get him started, or he'll be calling a hack to drive up to the house. I'll go home on a street car."

"So far so good," sighed Mr. Clayton to himself as he escaped from the station. "Jack is a deuced clever fellow, and I'll have to do something more for him. But the tug-of-war is yet to come. I've got to bribe a doctor, shut up the house for a day or two, and have all the ill-humor of two disappointed women to endure until this negro leaves town. Well, I'm sure my wife and Alice will back me up at any cost. No sacrifice is too great to escape having to entertain him; of course I have no prejudice against his color,—he can't help that,—but it is the *principle* of the thing. If we received him it would be a concession fatal to all my views and theories. And I am really doing him a kindness, for I'm sure that all the world could not make Alice and her mother treat him with anything but cold politeness. It'll be a great mortification to Alice, but I don't see how else I could have got out of it."

He boarded the first car that left the depot, and soon reached home. The house was lighted up, and through the lace curtains of the parlor windows he could see his wife and daughter, elegantly dressed, waiting to receive their distinguished visitor. He rang the bell impatiently, and a servant opened the door.

"The gentleman didn't come?" asked the maid.

"No," he said as he hung up his hat. This brought the ladies to the door.

"He didn't come?" they exclaimed. "What's the matter?"

"I'll tell you," he said. "Mary," this to the servant, a white girl, who stood in open-eyed curiosity, "we shan't need you any more to-night."

Then he went into the parlor, and, closing the door, told his story. When he reached the point where he had discovered the color of the honorable Mr. Brown, Miss Clayton caught her breath, and was on the verge of collapse.

"That nigger," said Mrs. Clayton indignantly, "can never set foot in this house. But what did you do with him?"

Mr. Clayton quickly unfolded his plan, and described the disposition he had made of the Congressman.

"It's an awful shame," said Mrs. Clayton. "Just think of the trouble and expense we have gone to! And poor Alice'll never get over it, for everybody knows he came to see her and that he's smitten with her. But you've done just right; we never would have been able to hold up our heads again if we had introduced a black man, even a Congressman, to the people that are invited here to-morrow night, as a sweetheart of Alice. Why, she wouldn't marry him if he was President of the United States and plated with gold an inch thick. The very idea!"

"Well," said Mr. Clayton, "then we've got to act quick. Alice must wrap up her throat—by the way, Alice, how *is* your throat?"

"It's sore," sobbed Alice, who had been in tears almost from her father's return, "and I don't care if I do have diphtheria and die, no, I don't!" and she wept on.

"Wrap up your throat and go to bed, and I'll go over to Doctor Pillsbury's and get a diphtheria card to nail up on the house. In the morning, first thing, we'll have to write notes recalling the invitations for to-morrow evening, and have them delivered by messenger boys. We were fools for not finding out all about this man from some one who knew, before we invited him here. Sadler don't know more than half he thinks he does, anyway. And we'll have to do this thing thoroughly, or our motives will be misconstrued, and people will say we are prejudiced and all that, when it is only a matter of principle with us."

The programme outlined above was carried out to the letter. The invitations were recalled, to the great disappointment of the invited guests. The family physician called several times during the day. Alice remained in bed, and the maid left without notice, in such a hurry that she forgot to take her best clothes.

Mr. Clayton himself remained at home. He had a telephone in the house, and was therefore in easy communication with his office, so that the business did not suffer materially by reason of his absence from the store. About ten o'clock in the morning a note came up from the hotel, expressing Mr. Brown's regrets and sympathy. Toward noon Mr. Clayton picked up the morning paper, which he had not theretofore had time to read, and was glancing over it casually, when his eye fell upon a column headed "A Colored Congressman." He read the article with astonishment that rapidly turned to chagrin and dismay. It was an interview describing the Congressman as a tall and shapely man, about thirty-five years old, with an olive complexion not noticeably darker than many a white man's, straight hair, and eyes as black as sloes.

"The bearing of this son of South Carolina reveals the polished manners of the Southern gentleman, and neither from his appearance nor his conversation would one suspect that the white blood which flows in his veins in such preponderating measure had ever been crossed by that of a darker race," wrote the reporter, who had received instructions at the office that for urgent business considerations the lake shipping interest wanted Representative Brown treated with marked consideration.

There was more of the article, but the introductory portion left Mr. Clayton in such a state of bewilderment that the paper fell from his hand. What was the meaning of it? Had he been mistaken? Obviously so, or else the reporter was wrong, which was manifestly improbable. When he had recovered himself somewhat, he picked up the newspaper and began reading where he had left off.

"Representative Brown traveled to Groveland in company with Bishop Jones of the African Methodist Jerusalem Church, who is *en route* to attend the general conference of his denomination at Detroit next week. The bishop, who came in while the writer was interviewing Mr. Brown, is a splendid type of the pure negro. He is said to be a man of great power among his people, which may easily be believed after one has looked upon his expressive countenance and heard him discuss the questions which affect the welfare of his church and his race."

Mr. Clayton stared at the paper. "'The bishop,'" he repeated, "'is a splendid type of the pure negro.' I must have mistaken the bishop for the Congressman! But how in the world did Jack get the thing balled up? I'll call up the store and demand an explanation of him.

"Jack," he asked, "what kind of a looking man was the fellow you gave the note to at the depot?"

"He was a very wicked-looking fellow, sir," came back the answer.

"He had a bàd eye, looked like a gambler, sir. I am not surprised that you didn't want to entertain him, even if he was a Congressman."

"What color was he—that's what I want to know—and what kind of hair did he have?"

"Why, he was about my complexion, sir, and had straight black hair."

The rules of the telephone company did not permit swearing over the line. Mr. Clayton broke the rules.

"Was there any one else with him?" he asked when he had relieved his mind.

"Yes, sir, Bishop Jones of the African Methodist Jerusalem Church was sitting there with him; they had traveled from Washington together. I drove the bishop to his stopping-place after I had left Mr. Brown at the hotel. I didn't suppose you'd mind."

Mr. Clayton fell into a chair, and indulged in thoughts unutterable. He folded up the paper and slipped it under the family Bible, where it was least likely to be soon discovered.

"I'll hide the paper, anyway," he groaned. "I'll never hear the last of this till my dying day, so I may as well have a few hours' respite. It's too late to go back, and we've got to play the farce out. Alice is really sick with disappointment, and to let her know this now would only make her worse. May be he'll leave town in a day or two, and then she'll be in condition to stand it. Such luck is enough to disgust a man with trying to do right and live up to his principles."

Time hung a little heavy on Mr. Clayton's hands during the day. His wife was busy with the housework. He answered several telephone calls about Alice's health, and called up the store occasionally to ask how the business was getting on. After lunch he lay down on a sofa and took a nap, from which he was aroused by the sound of the door-bell. He went to the door. The evening paper was lying on the porch, and the newsboy, who had not observed the diphtheria sign until after he had rung, was hurrying away as fast as his legs would carry him.

Mr. Clayton opened the paper and looked it through to see if there was any reference to the visiting Congressman. He found what he sought and more. An article on the local page contained a résumé of the information given in the morning paper, with the following additional paragraph:—

"A reporter, who called at the Forest Hill this morning to interview Representative Brown, was informed that the Congressman had been invited to spend the remainder of his time in Groveland as the guest of Mr. William Watkins, the proprietor of the popular livery establishment on Main Street. Mr. Brown will remain in the city several days, and a reception will be tendered him at Mr. Watkins's on Wednesday evening."

"That ends it," sighed Mr. Clayton. "The dove of peace will never again rest on my roof-tree."

But why dwell longer on the sufferings of Mr. Clayton, or attempt to describe the feelings or chronicle the remarks of his wife and daughter when they learned the facts in the case?

As to Representative Brown, he was made welcome in the hospitable home of Mr. William Watkins. There was a large and brilliant assemblage at the party on Wednesday evening, at which were displayed the costumes prepared for the Clayton reception. Mr. Brown took a fancy to Miss Lura Watkins, to whom, before the week was over, he became engaged to be married. Meantime poor Alice, the innocent victim of circumstances and principles, lay sick abed with a supposititious case of malignant diphtheria, and a real case of acute disappointment and chagrin.

"Oh, Jack!" exclaimed Alice, a few weeks later, on the way home from evening church in company with the young man, "what a dreadful thing it all was! And to think of that hateful Lura Watkins marrying the Congressman!"

The street was shaded by trees at the point where they were passing, and there was no one in sight. Jack put his arm around her waist, and, leaning over, kissed her.

"Never mind, dear," he said soothingly, "you still have your 'last chance' left, and I'll prove myself a better man than the Congressman."

Occasionally, at social meetings, when the vexed question of the future of the colored race comes up, as it often does, for discussion, Mr. Clayton may still be heard to remark sententiously:—

"What the white people of the United States need most, in dealing with this problem, is a higher conception of the brotherhood of man. For of one blood God made all the nations of the earth."

THE PASSING OF GRANDISON

1

WHEN IT is said that it was done to please a woman, there ought perhaps to be enough said to explain anything; for what a man will not do to please a woman is yet to be discovered. Nevertheless, it might be well to state a few preliminary facts to make it clear why young Dick Owens tried to run one of his father's negro men off to Canada.

In the early fifties, when the growth of anti-slavery sentiment and the constant drain of fugitive slaves into the North had so alarmed the slaveholders of the border States as to lead to the passage of the Fugitive Slave Law, a young white man from Ohio, moved by compassion for the sufferings of a certain bondman who happened to have a "hard master," essayed to help the slave to freedom. The attempt was discovered and frustrated; the abductor was tried and convicted for slave-stealing, and sentenced to a term of imprisonment in the penitentiary. His death, after the expiration of only a small part of the sentence, from cholera contracted while nursing stricken fellow prisoners, lent to the case a melancholy interest that made it famous in anti-slavery annals.

Dick Owens had attended the trial. He was a youth of about twenty-two, intelligent, handsome, and amiable, but extremely indolent, in a graceful and gentlemanly way; or, as old Judge Fenderson put it more than once, he was lazy as the Devil,—a mere figure of speech, of course, and not one that did justice to the Enemy of Mankind. When asked why he never did anything serious, Dick would good-naturedly reply, with a well-modulated drawl, that he didn't have to. His father was rich; there was but one other child, an unmarried daughter, who because of poor health would probably never marry, and Dick was therefore heir presumptive to a large estate. Wealth or social position he did not need to seek, for he was born to both. Charity Lomax had shamed him into studying law, but notwithstanding an hour or so a day spent at old Judge Fenderson's office, he did not make remarkable headway in his legal studies.

"What Dick needs," said the judge, who was fond of tropes, as became a scholar, and of horses, as was befitting a Kentuckian, "is the whip of necessity, or the spur of ambition. If he had either, he would soon need the snaffle to hold him back."

But all Dick required, in fact, to prompt him to the most remarkable thing he accomplished before he was twenty-five, was a mere suggestion from Charity Lomax. The story was never really known to but two persons until after the war, when it came out because it was a good story and there was no particular reason for its concealment.

Young Owens had attended the trial of this slave-stealer, or martyr,—either or both,—and, when it was over, had gone to call on Charity Lomax, and, while they sat on the veranda after sundown, had told her all about the trial. He was a good talker, as his career in later years disclosed, and described the proceedings very graphically.

"I confess," he admitted, "that while my principles were against the prisoner, my sympathies were on his side. It appeared that he was of good family, and that he had an old father and mother, respectable people, dependent upon him for support and comfort in their declining years. He had been led into the matter by pity for a negro whose master ought to have been run out of the county long ago for abusing his slaves. If it had been merely a question of old Sam Briggs's negro, nobody would have cared anything about it. But father and the rest of them stood on the principle of the thing, and told the judge so, and the fellow was sentenced to three years in the penitentiary."

Miss Lomax had listened with lively interest.

"I've always hated old Sam Briggs," she said emphatically, "ever since the time he broke a negro's leg with a piece of cordwood. When I hear of a cruel deed it makes the Quaker blood that came from my grandmother assert itself. Personally I wish that all Sam Briggs's negroes would run away. As for the young man, I regard him as a hero. He dared something for humanity. I could love a man who would take such chances for the sake of others."

"Could you love me, Charity, if I did something heroic?"

"You never will, Dick. You're too lazy for any use. You'll never do anything harder than playing cards or fox-hunting."

"Oh, come now, sweetheart! I've been courting you for a year, and it's the hardest work imaginable. Are you never going to love me?" he pleaded.

His hand sought hers, but she drew it back beyond his reach.

"I'll never love you, Dick Owens, until you have done something. When that time comes, I'll think about it."

"But it takes so long to do anything worth mentioning, and I don't want to wait. One must read two years to become a lawyer, and work five more to make a reputation. We shall both be gray by then."

"Oh, I don't know," she rejoined. "It doesn't require a lifetime for a man to prove that he is a man. This one did something, or at least tried to."

"Well, I'm willing to attempt as much as any other man. What do you want me to do, sweetheart? Give me a test."

"Oh, dear me!" said Charity, "I don't care what you *do*, so you do *something*. Really, come to think of it, why should I care whether you do anything or not?"

"I'm sure I don't know why you should, Charity," rejoined Dick humbly, "for I'm aware that I'm not worthy of it."

"Except that I do hate," she added, relenting slightly, "to see a really clever man so utterly lazy and good for nothing."

"Thank you, my dear; a word of praise from you has sharpened my wits already. I have an idea! Will you love me if *I* run a negro off to Canada?"

"What nonsense!" said Charity scornfully. "You must be losing your wits. Steal another man's slave, indeed, while your father owns a hundred!"

"Oh, there'll be no trouble about that," responded Dick lightly; "I'll run off one of the old man's; we've got too many anyway. It may not be quite as difficult as the other man found it, but it will be just as unlawful, and will demonstrate what I am capable of."

"Seeing's believing," replied Charity. "Of course, what you are talking about now is merely absurd. I'm going away for three weeks, to visit my aunt in Tennessee. If you're able to tell me, when I return, that you've done something to prove your quality, I'll—well, you may come and tell me about it."

II

Young Owens got up about nine o'clock next morning, and while making his toilet put some questions to his personal attendant, a rather bright looking young mulatto of about his own age.

"Tom," said Dick.

"Yas, Mars Dick," responded the servant.

"I'm going on a trip North. Would you like to go with me?"

Now, if there was anything that Tom would have liked to make, it was a trip North. It was something he had long contemplated in the abstract, but had never been able to muster up sufficient courage to attempt in the concrete. He was prudent enough, however, to dissemble his feelings.

"I wouldn't min' it, Mars Dick, ez long ez you'd take keer er me an' fetch me home all right."

Tom's eyes belied his words, however, and his young master felt well assured that Tom needed only a good opportunity to make him run away. Having a comfortable home, and a dismal prospect in case of failure, Tom was not likely to take any desperate chances; but young Owens was satisfied that in a free State but little persuasion would be required to lead Tom astray. With a very logical and characteristic desire to gain his end with the least necessary expenditure of effort, he decided to take Tom with him, if his father did not object.

Colonel Owens had left the house when Dick went to breakfast, so Dick did not see his father till luncheon.

"Father," he remarked casually to the colonel, over the fried chicken, "I'm feeling a trifle run down. I imagine my health would be improved somewhat by a little travel and change of scene."

"Why don't you take a trip North?" suggested his father. The colonel added to paternal affection a considerable respect for his son as the heir of a large estate. He himself had been "raised" in comparative poverty, and had laid the foundations of his fortune by hard work; and while he despised the ladder by which he had climbed, he could not entirely forget it, and unconsciously manifested, in his intercourse with his son, some of the poor man's deference toward the wealthy and well-born.

"I think I'll adopt your suggestion, sir," replied the son, "and run up to New York; and after I've been there awhile I may go on to Boston for a week or so. I've never been there, you know."

"There are some matters you can talk over with my factor in New York," rejoined the colonel, "and while you are up there among the Yankees, I hope you'll keep your eyes and ears open to find out what the rascally abolitionists are saying and doing. They're becoming altogether too active for our comfort, and entirely too many ungrateful niggers are running away. I hope the conviction of that fellow yesterday may discourage the rest of the breed. I'd just like to catch any one trying to run off one of my darkeys. He'd get short shrift; I don't think any Court would have a chance to try him."

"They are a pestiferous lot," assented Dick, "and dangerous to our institutions. But say, father, if I go North I shall want to take Tom with me."

Now, the colonel, while a very indulgent father, had pronounced views on the subject of negroes, having studied them, as he often said, for a great many years, and, as he asserted oftener still, understanding them perfectly. It is scarcely worth while to say, either, that he valued more highly than if he had inherited them the slaves he had toiled and schemed for.

"I don't think it safe to take Tom up North," he declared, with promptness and decision. "He's a good enough boy, but too smart to trust among those low-down abolitionists. I strongly suspect him of having learned to read, though I can't imagine how. I saw him with a newspaper the other day, and while he pretended to be looking at a woodcut, I'm almost sure he was reading the paper. I think it by no means safe to take him."

Dick did not insist, because he knew it was useless. The colonel would have obliged his son in any other matter, but his negroes were the outward and visible sign of his wealth and station, and therefore sacred to him.

"Whom do you think it safe to take?" asked Dick. "I suppose I'll have to have a body-servant."

"What's the matter with Grandison?" suggested the colonel. "He's handy enough, and I reckon we can trust him. He's too fond of good eating to risk losing his regular meals; besides, he's sweet on your mother's maid, Betty, and I've promised to let 'em get married before long. I'll have Grandison up, and we'll talk to him. Here, you boy Jack," called the colonel to a yellow youth in the next room who was catching flies and pulling their wings off to pass the time, "go down to the barn and tell Grandison to come here."

"Grandison," said the colonel, when the negro stood before him, hat in hand.

"Yas, marster."

"Haven't I always treated you right?"

"Yas, marster."

"Haven't you always got all you wanted to eat?"

"Yas, marster."

"And as much whiskey and tobacco as was good for you, Grandison?"

"Y-a-s, marster."

"I should just like to know, Grandison, whether you don't think yourself a great deal better off than those poor free negroes down by the plank road, with no kind master to look after them and no mistress to give them medicine when they're sick and—and"—

"Well, I sh'd jes' reckon I is better off, suh, dan dem low-down free niggers, suh! Ef anybody ax 'em who dey b'long ter, dey has ter say nobody, er e'se lie erbout it. Anybody ax me who I b'longs ter, I ain' got no 'casion ter be shame' ter tell 'em, no, suh, 'deed I ain', suh!"

The colonel was beaming. This was true gratitude, and his feudal heart thrilled at such appreciative homage. What cold-blooded, heartless monsters they were who would break up this blissful relationship of kindly protection on the one hand, of wise subordination and loyal dependence on the other! The colonel always became indignant at the mere thought of such wickedness.

"Grandison," the colonel continued, "your young master Dick is going North for a few weeks, and I am thinking of letting him take you along. I shall send you on this trip, Grandison, in order that you may take care of your young master. He will need some one to wait on him, and no one can ever do it so well as one of the boys brought up with him on the old plantation. I am going to trust him in your hands, and I'm sure you'll do your duty faithfully, and bring him back home safe and sound—to old Kentucky."

Grandison grinned. "Oh yas, marster, I'll take keer er young Mars Dick."

"I want to warn you, though, Grandison," continued the colonel impressively, "against these cussed abolitionists, who try to entice servants from their comfortable homes and their indulgent masters, from the blue skies, the green fields, and the warm sunlight of their Southern home, and send them away off yonder to Canada, a dreary country, where the woods are full of wildcats and wolves and bears, where the snow lies up to the eaves of the houses for six months of the year, and the cold is so severe that it freezes your breath and curdles your blood; and where, when runaway niggers get sick and can't work, they are turned out to starve and die, unloved and uncared for. I reckon, Grandison, that you have too much sense to permit yourself to be led astray by any such foolish and wicked people."

"'Deed, suh, I wouldn' 'low none er dem cussed, low-down abolitioners ter come nigh me, suh. I'd—I'd—would I be 'lowed ter hit 'em, suh?"

"Certainly, Grandison," replied the colonel, chuckling, "hit 'em as hard as you can. I reckon they'd rather like it. Begad, I believe they would! It would serve 'em right to be hit by a nigger!"

"Er ef I didn't hit 'em, suh," continued Grandison reflectively, "I'd tell Mars Dick, en *he'd* fex 'em. He'd smash de face off'n 'em suh, I jes' knows he would."

"Oh yes, Grandison, your young master will protect you. You need fear no harm while he is near."

"Dey won't try ter steal me, will dey, marster?" asked the negro, with sudden alarm.

"I don't know, Grandison," replied the colonel, lighting a fresh cigar. "They're a desperate set of lunatics, and there's no telling what they may resort to. But if you stick close to your young master, and remember always that he is your best friend, and understands your real needs, and has your true interests at heart, and if you will be careful to avoid strangers who try to talk to you, you'll stand a fair chance of getting back to your home and your friends. And if you please your master Dick, he'll buy you a present, and a string of beads for Betty to wear when you and she get married in the fall."

"Thanky, marster, thanky, suh," replied Grandison, oozing gratitude at every pore; "you is a good marster, to be sho', suh; yas, 'deed you is. You kin jes' bet me and Mars Dick gwine git 'long jes' lack I wuz own boy ter Mars Dick. En it won't be my fault ef he don' want me fer his boy all de time, w'en we come back home ag'in."

"All right, Grandison, you may go now. You needn't work any more to-day, and here's a piece of tobacco for you off my own plug."

"Thanky, marster, thanky, marster! You is de bes' marster any nigger ever had in dis worl'." And Grandison bowed and scraped and disappeared round the corner, his jaws closing around a large section of the colonel's best tobacco.

"You may take Grandison," said the colonel to his son. "I allow he's abolitionist-proof."

III

Richard Owens, Esq., and servant, from Kentucky, registered at the fashionable New York hostelry for Southerners in those days, a hotel where an atmosphere congenial to Southern institutions was sedulously maintained. But there were negro waiters in the dining-room, and mulatto bell-boys, and Dick had no doubt that Grandison, with the native gregariousness and garrulousness of his race, would foregather and palaver with them sooner or later, and Dick hoped that they would speedily inoculate him with the virus of freedom. For it was not Dick's intention to say anything to his servant about his plan to free him, for obvious reasons. To mention one of them, if Grandison should go away, and by legal process be recaptured, his young master's part in the matter would doubtless become known, which would be embarrassing to Dick, to say the least. If, on the other hand, he should merely give Grandison sufficient latitude, he had no doubt he would eventually lose him. For while not exactly skeptical about Grandison's perfervid loyalty, Dick had been a somewhat keen observer of human nature, in his own indolent way, and based his expectations upon the force of the example and argument that his servant could scarcely fail to encounter. Grandison should have a fair chance to become free by his own initiative; if it should become necessary to adopt other measures to get rid of him, it would be time enough to act when the necessity arose; and Dick Owens was not the youth to take needless trouble.

The young master renewed some acquaintances and made others, and spent a week or two very pleasantly in the best society of the metropolis, easily accessible to a wealthy, well-bred young Southerner, with proper introductions. Young women smiled on him, and young men of convivial habits pressed their hospitalities; but the memory of Charity's sweet, strong face and clear blue eyes made him proof against the blandishments of the one sex and the persuasions of the other. Meanwhile he kept Grandison supplied with pocket-money, and left him mainly to his own devices. Every night when Dick came in he hoped he might have to wait upon himself, and every morning he looked forward with pleasure to the prospect of making his toilet unaided. His hopes, however, were doomed to disappointment, for every night when he came in Grandison was on hand with a bootjack, and a nightcap mixed for his young master as the colonel had taught him to mix it, and every morning Grandison appeared with his master's boots blacked and his clothes brushed, and laid his linen out for the day.

"Grandison," said Dick one morning, after finishing his toilet, "this is the chance of your life to go around among your own people and see how they live. Have you met any of them?"

"Yas, suh, I's seen some of 'em. But I don' keer nuffin fer 'em, suh. Dey're diffe'nt f'm de niggers down ou' way. Dey 'lows dey're free, but dey ain' got sense 'nuff ter know dey ain' half as well off as dey would be down Souf, whar dey'd be 'preciated."

When two weeks had passed without any apparent effect of evil example upon Grandison, Dick resolved to go on to Boston, where he thought the atmosphere might prove more favorable to his ends. After he had been at the Revere House for a day or two without losing Grandison, he decided upon slightly different tactics.

Having ascertained from a city directory the addresses of several well-known abolitionists, he wrote them each a letter something like this:—

DEAR FRIEND AND BROTHER:—
A wicked slaveholder from Kentucky, stopping at the Revere House, has dared to insult the liberty-loving people of Boston by bringing his slave into their midst. Shall this be tolerated? Or shall steps be taken in the name of liberty to rescue a fellow-man from bondage? For obvious reasons I can only sign myself,
                                                 A FRIEND OF HUMANITY.

That his letter might have an opportunity to prove effective, Dick made it a point to send Grandison away from the hotel on various errands. On one of these occasions Dick watched him for quite a distance down the street. Grandison had scarcely left the hotel when a long-haired, sharp-featured man came out behind him, followed him, soon overtook him, and kept along beside him until they turned the next corner. Dick's hopes were roused by this spectacle, but sank correspondingly when Grandison returned to the hotel. As Grandison said nothing about the encounter, Dick hoped there might be some self-consciousness behind this unexpected reticence, the results of which might develop later on.

But Grandison was on hand again when his master came back to the hotel at night, and was in attendance again in the morning, with hot water, to assist at his master's toilet. Dick sent him on further errands from day to day, and upon one occasion came squarely up to him—inadvertently of course—while Grandison was engaged in conversation with a young white man in clerical garb. When Grandison saw Dick approaching, he edged away from the preacher and hastened toward his master, with a very evident expression of relief upon his countenance.

"Mars Dick," he said, "dese yer abolitioners is jes' pesterin' de life out er me tryin' ter git me ter run away. I don' pay no 'tention ter 'em, but dey riles me so sometimes dat I'm feared I'll hit some of 'em some er dese days, an' dat mought git me inter trouble. I ain' said nuffin' ter you 'bout it, Mars Dick, fer I didn' wanter 'sturb yo' min'; but I don' like it, suh; no, suh, I don'! Is we gwine back home 'fo' long, Mars Dick?"

"We'll be going back soon enough," replied Dick somewhat shortly, while he inwardly cursed the stupidity of a slave who could be free and would not, and registered a secret vow that if he were unable to get rid of Grandison without assassinating him, and were therefore compelled to take him back to Kentucky, he would see that Grandison got a taste of an article of slavery that would make him regret his wasted opportunities. Meanwhile he determined to tempt his servant yet more strongly.

"Grandison," he said next morning, "I'm going away for a day or two, but I shall leave you here. I shall lock up a hundred dollars in this drawer and give you the key. If you need any of it, use it and enjoy yourself,—spend it all if you like,—for this is probably the last chance you'll have for some time to be in a free State, and you'd better enjoy your liberty while you may."

When he came back a couple of days later and found the faithful Grandison at his post, and the hundred dollars intact, Dick felt seriously annoyed. His vexation was increased by the fact that he could not express his feelings adequately. He did not even scold Grandison; how could he, indeed, find fault with one who so sensibly recognized his true place in the economy of civilization, and kept it with such touching fidelity?

"I can't say a thing to him," groaned Dick. "He deserves a leather medal, made out of his own hide tanned. I reckon I'll write to father and let him know what a model servant he has given me."

He wrote his father a letter which made the colonel swell with pride and pleasure. "I really think," the colonel observed to one of his friends, "that Dick ought to have the nigger interviewed by the Boston papers, so that they may see how contented and happy our darkeys really are."

Dick also wrote a long letter to Charity Lomax, in which he said, among many other things, that if she knew how hard he was working, and under what difficulties, to accomplish something serious for her sake, she would no longer keep him in suspense, but overwhelm him with love and admiration.

Having thus exhausted without result the more obvious methods of getting rid of Grandison, and diplomacy having also proved a failure, Dick was forced to consider more radical measures. Of course he might run away himself, and abandon Grandison, but this would be merely to leave him in the United States, where he was still a slave, and where, with his notions of loyalty, he would speedily be reclaimed. It was necessary, in order to accomplish the purpose of his trip to the North, to leave Grandison permanently in Canada, where he would be legally free.

"I might extend my trip to Canada," he reflected, "but that would be too palpable. I have it! I'll visit Niagara Falls on the way home, and lose him on the Canada side. When he once realizes that he is actually free, I'll warrant that he'll stay."

So the next day saw them westward bound, and in due course of time, by the somewhat slow conveyances of the period, they found themselves at Niagara. Dick walked and drove about the Falls for several days, taking Grandison along with him on most occasions. One morning they stood on the Canadian side, watching the wild whirl of the waters below them.

"Grandison," said Dick, raising his voice above the roar of the cataract, "do you know where you are now?"

"I's wid you, Mars Dick; dat's all I keers."

"You are now in Canada, Grandison, where your people go when they run away from their masters. If you wished, Grandison, you might walk away from me this very minute, and I could not lay my hand upon you to take you back."

Grandison looked around uneasily.

"Let's go back ober de ribber, Mars Dick. I's feared I'll lose you ovuh heah, an' den I won' hab no marster, an' won' nebber be able to git back home no mo'."

Discouraged, but not yet hopeless, Dick said, a few minutes later,—

"Grandison, I'm going up the road a bit, to the inn over yonder. You stay here until I return. I'll not be gone a great while."

Grandison's eyes opened wide and he looked somewhat fearful.

"Is dey any er dem dadblasted abolitioners roun' heah, Mars Dick?"

"I don't imagine that there are," replied his master, hoping there might be. "But I'm not afraid of *your* running away, Grandison. I only wish I were," he added to himself.

Dick walked leisurely down the road to where the white-washed inn, built of stone, with true British solidity, loomed up through the trees by the roadside. Arrived there, he ordered a glass of ale and a sandwich, and took a seat at a table by a window, from which he could see Grandison in the distance. For a while he hoped that the seed he had sown might have fallen on fertile ground, and that Grandison, relieved from the restraining power of a master's eye, and finding himself in a free country, might get up and walk away; but the hope was vain, for Grandison remained faithfully at his post, awaiting his master's return. He had seated himself on a broad flat stone, and, turning his eyes away from the grand and awe-inspiring spectacle that lay close at hand, was looking anxiously toward the inn where his master sat cursing his ill-timed fidelity.

By and by a girl came into the room to serve his order, and Dick very naturally glanced at her; and as she was young and pretty and remained in attendance, it was some minutes before he looked for Grandison. When he did so his faithful servant had disappeared.

To pay his reckoning and go away without the change was a matter quickly accomplished. Retracing his footsteps toward the Falls, he saw, to his great disgust, as he approached the spot where he had left Grandison, the familiar form of his servant stretched out on the ground, his face to the sun, his mouth open, sleeping the time away, oblivious alike to the grandeur of the scenery, the thunderous roar of the cataract, or the insidious voice of sentiment.

"Grandison," soliloquized his master, as he stood gazing down at his ebony encumbrance, "I do not deserve to be an American citizen; I ought not to have the advantages I possess over you; and I certainly am not worthy of Charity Lomax, if I am not smart enough to get rid of you. I have an idea! You shall yet be free, and I will be the instrument of your deliverance. Sleep on, faithful and affectionate servitor, and dream of the blue grass and the bright skies of old Kentucky, for it is only in your dreams that you will ever see them again!"

Dick retraced his footsteps toward the inn. The young woman chanced to look out of the window and saw the handsome young gentleman she had waited on a few minutes before, standing in the road a short distance away, apparently engaged in earnest conversation with a colored man employed as hostler for the inn. She thought she saw something pass from the white man to the other, but at that moment her duties called her away from the window, and when she looked out again the young gentleman had disappeared, and the hostler, with two other young men of the neighborhood, one white and one colored, was walking rapidly toward the Falls.

IV

Dick made the journey homeward alone, and as rapidly as the conveyances of the day would permit. As he drew near home his conduct in going back without Grandison took on a more serious aspect than it had borne at any previous time, and although he had prepared the colonel by a letter sent several days ahead, there was still the prospect of a bad quarter of an hour with him; not, indeed, that his father would upbraid him, but he was likely to make searching inquiries. And notwithstanding the vein of quiet recklessness that had carried Dick through his preposterous scheme, he was a very poor liar, having rarely had occasion or inclination to tell anything but the truth. Any reluctance to meet his father was more than offset, however, by a stronger force drawing him homeward, for Charity Lomax must long since have returned from her visit to her aunt in Tennessee.

Dick got off easier than he had expected. He told a straight story, and a truthful one, so far as it went.

The colonel raged at first, but rage soon subsided into anger, and anger moderated into annoyance, and annoyance into a sort of garrulous sense of injury. The colonel thought he had been hardly used; he had trusted this negro, and he had broken faith. Yet, after all, he did not blame Grandison so much as he did the abolitionists, who were undoubtedly at the bottom of it.

As for Charity Lomax, Dick told her, privately of course, that he had run his father's man, Grandison, off to Canada, and left him there.

"Oh, Dick," she had said with shuddering alarm, "what have you done? If they knew it they'd send you to the penitentiary, like they did that Yankee."

"But they don't know it," he had replied seriously; adding, with an injured tone, "you don't seem to appreciate my heroism like you did that of the Yankee; perhaps it's because I wasn't caught and sent to the penitentiary. I thought you wanted me to do it."

"Why, Dick Owens!" she exclaimed. "You know I never dreamed of any such outrageous proceeding.

"But I presume I'll have to marry you," she concluded, after some insistence on Dick's part, "if only to take care of you. You are too reckless for anything; and a man who goes chasing all over the North, being entertained by New York and Boston society and having negroes to throw away, needs some one to look after him."

"It's a most remarkable thing," replied Dick fervently, "that your views correspond exactly with my profoundest convictions. It proves beyond question that we were made for one another."

They were married three weeks later. As each of them had just returned from a journey, they spent their honeymoon at home.

A week after the wedding they were seated, one afternoon, on the piazza of the colonel's house, where Dick had taken his bride, when a negro from the yard ran down the lane and threw open the big gate for the colonel's buggy to enter. The colonel was not alone. Beside him, ragged and travel-stained, bowed with weariness and upon his face a haggard look that told of hardship and privation, sat the lost Grandison.

The colonel alighted at the steps.

"Take the lines, Tom," he said to the man who had opened the gate, "and drive round to the barn. Help Grandison down,—poor devil, he's so stiff he can hardly move!—and get a tub of water and wash him and rub him down, and feed him, and give him a big drink of whiskey, and then let him come round and see his young master and his new mistress."

The colonel's face wore an expression compounded of joy and indignation,—joy at the restoration of a valuable piece of property; indignation for reasons he proceeded to state.

"It's astounding, the depths of depravity the human heart is capable of! I was coming along the road three miles away, when I heard some one call me from the roadside. I pulled up the mare, and who should come out of the woods but Grandison. The poor nigger could hardly crawl along, with the help of a broken limb. I was never more astonished in my life. You could have knocked me down with a feather. He seemed pretty far gone,—he could hardly talk above a whisper,—and I had to give him a mouthful of whiskey to brave him up so he could tell his story. It's just as I thought from the beginning, Dick; Grandison had no notion of running away; he knew when he was well off, and where his friends were. All the persuasions of abolition liars and runaway niggers did not move him. But the desperation of those fanatics knew no bounds; their guilty consciences gave them no rest. They got the notion somehow that Grandison belonged to a nigger-catcher, and had been brought North as a spy to help capture ungrateful runaway servants. They actually kidnapped him—just think of it!—and gagged him and bound him and threw him rudely into a wagon, and carried him into the gloomy depths of a Canadian forest, and locked him in a lonely hut, and fed him on bread and water for three weeks. One of the scoundrels wanted to kill him, and persuaded the others that it ought to be done; but they got to quarreling about how they should do it, and before they had their minds made up Grandison escaped, and, keeping his back steadily to the North Star, made his way, after suffering incredible hardships, back to the old plantation, back to his master, his friends, and his home. Why, it's as good as one of Scott's novels! Mr. Simms or some other one of our Southern authors ought to write it up."

"Don't you think, sir," suggested Dick, who had calmly smoked his cigar throughout the colonel's animated recital, "that that kidnapping yarn sounds a little improbable? Isn't there some more likely explanation?"

"Nonsense, Dick; it's the gospel truth! Those infernal abolitionists are capable of anything—everything! Just think of their locking the poor, faithful nigger up, beating him, kicking him, depriving him of his liberty, keeping him on bread and water for three long, lonesome weeks, and he all the time pining for the old plantation!"

There were almost tears in the colonel's eyes at the picture of Grandison's sufferings that he conjured up. Dick still professed to be slightly skeptical, and met Charity's severely questioning eye with bland unconsciousness.

The colonel killed the fatted calf for Grandison, and for two or three weeks the returned wanderer's life was a slave's dream of pleasure. His fame spread throughout the county, and the colonel gave him a permanent place among the house servants, where he could always have him conveniently at hand to relate his adventures to admiring visitors.

About three weeks after Grandison's return the colonel's faith in sable humanity was rudely shaken, and its foundations almost broken up. He came near losing his belief in the fidelity of the negro to his master,—the servile virtue most highly prized and most sedulously cultivated by the colonel and his kind. One Monday morning Grandison was missing. And not only Grandison, but his wife, Betty the maid; his mother, aunt Eunice; his father, uncle Ike; his brothers, Tom and John, and his little sister, Elsie, were likewise absent from the plantation; and a hurried search and inquiry in the neighborhood resulted in no information as to their whereabouts. So much valuable property could not be lost without an effort to recover it, and the wholesale nature of the transaction carried consternation to the hearts of those whose ledgers were chiefly bound in black. Extremely energetic measures were taken by the colonel and his friends. The fugitives were traced, and followed from point to point, on their northward run through Ohio. Several times the hunters were close upon their heels, but the magnitude of the escaping party begot unusual vigilance on the part of those who sympathized with the fugitives, and strangely enough, the underground railroad seemed to have had its tracks cleared and signals set for this particular train. Once, twice, the colonel thought he had them, but they slipped through his fingers.

One last glimpse he caught of his vanishing property, as he stood, accompanied by a United States marshal, on a wharf at a port on the south shore of Lake Erie. On the stern of a small steamboat which was receding rapidly from the wharf, with her nose pointing toward Canada, there stood a group of familiar dark faces, and the look they cast backward was not one of longing for the fleshpots of Egypt. The colonel saw Grandison point him out to one of the crew of the vessel, who waved his hand derisively toward the colonel. The latter shook his fist impotently—and the incident was closed.

BAXTER'S *PROCRUSTES*

BAXTER'S *PROCRUSTES* is one of the publications of the Bodleian Club. The Bodleian Club is composed of gentlemen of culture, who are interested in books and book-collecting. It was named, very obviously, after the famous library of the same name, and not only became in our city a sort of shrine for local worshippers of fine bindings and rare editions, but was visited occasionally by pilgrims from afar. The Bodleian has entertained Mark Twain, Joseph Jefferson, and other literary and histrionic celebrities. It possesses quite a collection of personal mementos of distinguished authors, among them a paperweight which once belonged to Goethe, a lead pencil used by Emerson, an autograph letter of Matthew Arnold, and a chip from a tree felled by Mr. Gladstone. Its library contains a number of rare books, including a fine collection on chess, of which game several of the members are enthusiastic devotees.

The activities of the club are not, however, confined entirely to books. We have a very handsome clubhouse, and much taste and discrimination have been exercised in its adornment. There are many good paintings, including the portraits of the various presidents of the club, which adorn the entrance hall. After books, perhaps the most distinctive feature of the club is our collection of pipes. In a large rack in the smoking-room — really a superfluity, since smoking is permitted all over the house — is as complete an assortment of pipes as perhaps exists in the civilized world. Indeed, it is an unwritten rule of the club that no one is eligible for membership who cannot produce a new variety of pipe, which is filed with his application for membership, and, if he passes, deposited with the club collection, he, however, retaining the title in himself. Once a year, upon the anniversary of the death of Sir Walter Raleigh, who, it will be remembered, first introduced tobacco into England, the full membership of the club, as a rule, turns out. A large supply of the very best smoking mixture is laid in. At nine o'clock sharp each member takes his pipe from the rack, fills it with tobacco, and then the whole club, with the president at the head, all smoking furiously, march in solemn procession from room to room, upstairs and downstairs, making the tour of the clubhouse and returning to the smoking-room. The president then delivers an address, and each member is called upon to say something, either by way of a quotation or an original sentiment, in praise of the virtues of nicotine. This ceremony—facetiously known as "hitting the pipe"—being thus concluded, the membership pipes are carefully cleaned out and replaced in the club rack.

As I have said, however, the *raison d'être* of the club, and the feature upon which its fame chiefly rests, is its collection of rare books, and of these by far the most interesting are its own publications. Even its catalogues are works of art, published in numbered editions, and sought by libraries and book-collectors. Early in its history it began the occasional publication of books which should meet the club standard—books in which emphasis should be laid upon the qualities that make a book valuable in the eyes of collectors. Of these, age could not, of course, be imparted, but in the matter of fine and curious bindings, of hand-made linen papers, of uncut or deckle edges, of wide margins and limited editions, the club could control its own publications. The matter of contents was, it must be confessed, a less important consideration. At first it was felt by the publishing committee that nothing but the finest products of the human mind should be selected for enshrinement in the beautiful volumes which the club should issue. The length of the work was an important consideration—long things were not compatible with wide margins and graceful slenderness. For instance, we brought out Coleridge's *Ancient Mariner*, an essay by Emerson, and another by Thoreau. Our *Rubáiyát of Omar Khayyám* was Heron-Allen's translation of the original manuscript in the Bodleian Library at Oxford, which though less poetical than FitzGerald's was not so common. Several years ago we began to publish the works of our own members. Bascom's *Essay on Pipes* was a very creditable performance. It was published in a limited edition of one hundred copies, and since it had not previously appeared elsewhere and was copyrighted by the club, it was sufficiently rare to be valuable for that reason. The second publication of local origin was Baxter's *Procrustes*.

I have omitted to say that once or twice a year, at a meeting of which notice has been given, an auction is held at the Bodleian. The members of the club send in their duplicate copies, or books they for any reason wish to dispose of, which are auctioned off to the highest bidder. At these sales, which are well attended, the club's publications have of recent years formed the leading feature. Three years ago, number three of Bascom's *Essay on Pipes* sold for fifteen dollars—the original cost at publication was one dollar and seventy-five cents. Later in the evening an uncut copy of the same brought thirty dollars. At the next auction the price of the cut copy was run up to twenty-five dollars, while the uncut copy was knocked down at seventy-five dollars. The club had always appreciated the value of uncut copies, but this financial endorsement enhanced their desirability immensely. This rise in the *Essay on Pipes* was not without a sympathetic effect upon all the club publications. The Emerson essay rose from three dollars to seventeen, and the Thoreau, being by an author less widely read, and by his own confession commercially unsuccessful, brought a somewhat higher figure. The prices, thus inflated, were not permitted to come down appreciably. Since every member of the club possessed one or more of these valuable editions, they were all manifestly interested in keeping up the price. The publication, however, which brought the highest prices, and, but for the sober second thought, might have wrecked the whole system, was Baxter's *Procrustes*.

Baxter was, perhaps, the most scholarly member of the club. A graduate of Harvard, he had traveled extensively, had read widely, and while not so enthusiastic a collector as some of us, possessed as fine a private library as any man of his age in the city. He was about thirty-five when he joined the club, and apparently some bitter experience—some disappointment in love or ambition—had left its mark upon his character. With light, curly hair, fair complexion and gray eyes, one would have expected Baxter to be genial of temper, with a tendency toward wordiness of speech. But though he had occasional flashes of humor, his ordinary demeanor was characterized by a mild cynicism, which, with his gloomy pessimistic philosophy, so foreign to the temperament that should accompany his physical type, could only be accounted for upon the hypothesis of some secret sorrow such as I have suggested. What it might be no one knew. He had means and social position, and was an uncommonly handsome man. The fact that he remained unmarried at thirty-five furnished some support for the theory of a disappointment in love, though this the several intimates of Baxter who belonged to the club were not able to verify.

It had occurred to me, in a vague way, that perhaps Baxter might be an unsuccessful author. That he was a poet we knew very well, and typewritten copies of his verses had occasionally circulated among us. But Baxter had always expressed such a profound contempt for modern literature, had always spoken in terms of such unmeasured pity for the slaves of the pen, who were dependent upon the whim of an undiscriminating public for recognition and a livelihood, that no one of us had ever suspected him of aspirations toward publication, until, as I have said, it occurred to me one day that Baxter's attitude with regard to publication might be viewed in the light of effect as well as of cause—that his scorn of publicity might as easily arise from failure to achieve it, as his never having published might be due to his preconceived disdain of the vulgar popularity which one must share with the pugilist or balloonist of the hour.

The notion of publishing Baxter's *Procrustes* did not emanate from Baxter—I must do him the justice to say this. But he had spoken to several of the fellows about the theme of his poem, until the notion that Baxter was at work upon something fine had become pretty well disseminated throughout our membership. He would occasionally read brief passages to a small coterie of friends in the sitting room or library—never more than ten lines at once, or to more than five people at a time—and these excerpts gave at least a few of us a pretty fair idea of the motive and scope of the poem. As I, for one, gathered it, it was quite along the line of Baxter's philosophy. Society was the Procrustes which, like the Greek bandit of old, caught every man born into the world, and endeavored to fit him to some preconceived standard, generally to the one for which he was least adapted. The world was full of men and women who were merely square pegs in round holes, and vice versa. Most marriages were unhappy because the contracting parties were not properly mated. Religion was mostly superstition, science for the most part sciolism, popular education merely a means of forcing the stupid and repressing the bright, so that all the youth of the rising generation might conform to the same dull, dead level of democratic mediocrity. Life would soon become so monotonously uniform and so uniformly monotonous as to be scarce worth the living.

It was Smith, I think, who first proposed that the club publish Baxter's *Procrustes*. The poet himself did not seem enthusiastic when the subject was broached; he demurred for some little time, protesting that the poem was not worthy of publication. But when it was proposed that the edition be limited to fifty copies, he agreed to consider the proposition. When I suggested, having in mind my secret theory of Baxter's failure in authorship, that the edition would at least be in the hands of friends, that it would be difficult for a hostile critic to secure a copy, and that if it should not achieve success from a literary point of view, the extent of the failure would be limited to the size of the edition, Baxter was visibly impressed. When the literary committee at length decided to request formally of Baxter the privilege of publishing his *Procrustes*, he consented, with evident reluctance, upon condition that he should supervise the printing, binding, and delivery of the books, merely submitting to the committee, in advance, the manuscript, and taking their views in regard to the book-making.

The manuscript was duly presented to the literary committee. Baxter having expressed the desire that the poem not be read aloud at a meeting of the club, as was the custom, since he wished it to be given to the world clad in suitable garb, the committee went even farther. Having entire confidence in Baxter's taste and scholarship, they, with great delicacy, refrained from even reading the manuscript, contenting themselves with Baxter's statement of the general theme and the topics grouped under it. The details of the book-making, however, were gone into thoroughly. The paper was to be of hand-made linen, from the Kelmscott Mills; the type black-letter, with rubricated initials. The cover, which was Baxter's own selection, was to be of dark green morocco, with a cap-and-bells border in red inlays, and doublures of maroon morocco with a blind-tooled design. Baxter was authorized to contract with the printer and superintend the publication. The whole edition of fifty numbered copies was to be disposed of at auction, in advance, to the highest bidder, only one copy to each, the proceeds to be devoted to paying for the printing and binding, the remainder, if any, to go into the club treasury, and Baxter himself to receive one copy by way of remuneration. Baxter was inclined to protest at this, on the ground that his copy would probably be worth more than the royalties on the edition, at the usual ten per cent, would amount to, but was finally prevailed upon to accept an author's copy.

While the *Procrustes* was under consideration, someone read, at one of our meetings, a note from some magazine which stated that a sealed copy of a new translation of Campanella's *Sonnets*, published by the Grolier Club, had been sold for three hundred dollars. This impressed the members greatly. It was a novel idea. A new work might thus be enshrined in a sort of holy of holies, which, if the collector so desired, could be forever sacred from the profanation of any vulgar or unappreciative eye. The possessor of such a treasure could enjoy it by the eye of imagination, having at the same time the exaltation of grasping what was for others the unattainable. The literary committee were so impressed with this idea that they presented it to Baxter in regard to the *Procrustes*. Baxter making no objection, the subscribers who might wish their copies delivered sealed were directed to notify the author. I sent in my name. A fine book, after all, was an investment, and if there was any way of enhancing its rarity, and therefore its value, I was quite willing to enjoy such an advantage.

When the *Procrustes* was ready for distribution, each subscriber received his copy by mail, in a neat pasteboard box. Each number was wrapped in a thin and transparent but very strong paper, through which the cover design and toolings were clearly visible. The number of the copy was endorsed upon the wrapper, the folds of which were securely fastened at each end with sealing-wax, upon which was impressed, as a guaranty of its inviolateness, the monogram of the club.

At the next meeting of the Bodleian a great deal was said about the *Procrustes*, and it was unanimously agreed that no finer specimen of book-making had ever been published by the club. By a curious coincidence, no one had brought his copy with him, and the two club copies had not yet been received from the binder, who, Baxter had reported, was retaining them for some extra fine work. Upon resolution, offered by a member who had not subscribed for the volume, a committee of three was appointed to review the *Procrustes* at the next literary meeting of the club. Of this committee it was my doubtful fortune to constitute one.

In pursuance of my duty in the premises, it of course became necessary for me to read the *Procrustes*. In all probability I should have cut my own copy for this purpose, had not one of the club auctions intervened between my appointment and the date set for the discussion of the *Procrustes*. At this meeting a copy of the book, still sealed, was offered for sale and bought by a non-subscriber for the unprecedented price of one hundred and fifty dollars. After this a proper regard for my own interests would not permit me to spoil my copy by opening it, and I was therefore compelled to procure my information concerning the poem from some other source. As I had no desire to appear mercenary, I said nothing about my own copy, and made no attempt to borrow. I did, however, casually remark to Baxter that I should like to look at his copy of the proof sheets, since I wished to make some extended quotations for my review, and would rather not trust my copy to a typist for that purpose. Baxter assured me, with every evidence of regret, that he had considered them of so little importance that he had thrown them into the fire. This indifference of Baxter to literary values struck me as just a little overdone. The proof sheets of "Hamlet," corrected in Shakespeare's own hand, would be well-nigh priceless.

At the next meeting of the club I observed that Thompson and Davis, who were with me on the reviewing committee, very soon brought up the question of the *Procrustes* in conversation in the smoking-room, and seemed anxious to get from the members their views concerning Baxter's production, I supposed upon the theory that the appreciation of any book review would depend more or less upon the degree to which it reflected the opinion of those to whom the review should be presented. I presumed, of course, that Thompson and Davis had each read the book—they were among the subscribers—and I was desirous of getting their point of view.

"What do you think," I inquired, "of the passage on Social Systems?" I have forgotten to say that the poem was in blank verse, and divided into parts, each with an appropriate title.

"Well," replied Davis, it seemed to me a little cautiously, "it is not exactly Spencerian, although it squints at the Spencerian view, with a slight deflection toward Hegelianism. I should consider it an harmonious fusion of the best views of all the modern philosophers, with a strong Baxterian flavor."

"Yes," said Thompson, "the charm of the chapter lies in this very quality. The style is an emanation from Baxter's own intellect—he has written himself into the poem. By knowing Baxter we are able to appreciate the book, and after having read the book we feel that we are so much the more intimately acquainted with Baxter—the real Baxter."

Baxter had come in during this colloquy and was standing by the fireplace smoking a pipe. I was not exactly sure whether the faint smile which marked his face was a token of pleasure or cynicism; it was Baxterian, however, and I had already learned that Baxter's opinions upon any subject were not to be gathered always from his facial expression. For instance, when the club porter's crippled child died, Baxter remarked, it seemed to me unfeelingly, that the poor little devil was doubtless better off, and that the porter himself had certainly been relieved of a burden; and only a week later the porter told me in confidence that Baxter had paid for an expensive operation, undertaken in the hope of prolonging the child's life. I therefore drew no conclusions from Baxter's somewhat enigmatical smile. He left the room at this point in the conversation, somewhat to my relief.

"By the way, Jones," said Davis, addressing me, "are you impressed by Baxter's views on Degeneration?"

Having often heard Baxter express himself upon the general downward tendency of modern civilization, I felt safe in discussing his views in a broad and general manner.

"I think," I replied, "that they are in harmony with those of Schopenhauer, without his bitterness; with those of Nordau, without his flippancy. His materialism is Haeckel's, presented with something of the charm of Omar Khayyam."

"Yes," chimed in Davis, "it answers the strenuous demand of our day—dissatisfaction with an unjustified optimism—and voices for us the courage of human philosophy facing the unknown."

I had a vague recollection of having read something like this somewhere, but so much has been written that one can scarcely discuss any subject of importance without unconsciously borrowing, now and then, the thoughts or the language of others. Quotation, like imitation, is a superior grade of flattery.

"The *Procrustes*," said Thompson, to whom the metrical review had been apportioned, "is couched in sonorous lines, of haunting melody and charm; and yet so closely interrelated as to be scarcely quotable with justice to the author. To be appreciated the poem should be read as a whole—I shall say as much in my review. What shall you say of the letter-press?" he concluded, addressing me. I was supposed to discuss the technical excellence of the volume from the connoisseur's viewpoint.

"The setting," I replied judicially, "is worthy of the gem. The dark green cover, elaborately tooled, the old English lettering, the heavy linen paper, mark this as one of our very choicest publications. The letter-press is of course De Vinne's best—there is nothing better on this side of the Atlantic. The text is a beautiful, slender stream, meandering gracefully through a wide meadow of margin."

For some reason I left the room for a minute. As I stepped into the hall, I almost ran into Baxter, who was standing near the door, facing a hunting print, of a somewhat humorous character, hung upon the wall, and smiling with an immensely pleased expression.

"What a ridiculous scene!" he remarked. "Look at that fat old squire on that tall hunter! I'll wager dollars to doughnuts that he won't get over the first fence!"

It was a very good bluff, but did not deceive me. Under his mask of unconcern, Baxter was anxious to learn what we thought of his poem and had stationed himself in the hall that he might overhear our discussion without embarrassing us by his presence. He had covered up his delight at our appreciation by this simulated interest in the hunting print.

When the night came for the review of the *Procrustes* there was a large attendance of members, and several visitors, among them a young English cousin of one of the members, on his first visit to the United States; some of us had met him at other clubs, and in society, and had found him a very jolly boy, with a youthful exuberance of spirits and a naive ignorance of things American that made his views refreshing and, at times, amusing.

The critical essays were well considered, if a trifle vague. Baxter received credit for poetic skill of a high order.

"Our brother Baxter," said Thompson, "should no longer bury his talent in a napkin. This gem, of course, belongs to the club, but the same brain from which issued this exquisite emanation can produce others to inspire and charm an appreciative world."

"The author's view of life," said Davis, "as expressed in these beautiful lines, will help us to fit our shoulders for the heavy burden of life, by bringing to our realization those profound truths of philosophy which find hope in despair and pleasure in pain. When he shall see fit to give to the wider world, in fuller form, the thoughts of which we have been vouchsafed this foretaste, let us hope that some little ray of his fame may rest upon the Bodleian, from which can never be taken away the proud privilege of saying that he was one of its members."

I then pointed out the beauties of the volume as a piece of book-making. I knew, from conversation with the publication committee, the style of type and rubrication, and could see the cover through the wrapper of my sealed copy. The dark green morocco, I said, in summing up, typified the author's serious view of life, as a thing to be endured as patiently as might be. The cap-and-bells border was significant of the shams by which the optimist sought to delude himself into the view that life was a desirable thing. The intricate blind-tooling of the doublure shadowed forth the blind fate which left us in ignorance of our future and our past, or of even what the day itself might bring forth. The black-letter type, with rubricated initials, signified a philosophic pessimism enlightened by the conviction that in duty one might find, after all, an excuse for life and a hope for humanity. Applying this test to the club, this work, which might be said to represent all that the Bodleian stood for, was in itself sufficient to justify the club's existence. If the Bodleian had done nothing else, if it should do nothing more, it had produced a masterpiece.

There was a sealed copy of the *Procrustes*, belonging, I believe, to one of the committee, lying on the table by which I stood, and I had picked it up and held it in my hand for a moment, to emphasize one of my periods, but had laid it down immediately. I noted, as I sat down, that young Hankin, our English visitor, who sat on the other side of the table, had picked up the volume and was examining it with interest. When the last review was read, and the generous applause had subsided, there were cries for Baxter.

"Baxter! Baxter! Author! Author!"

Baxter had been sitting over in a corner during the reading of the reviews, and had succeeded remarkably well, it seemed to me, in concealing, under his mask of cynical indifference, the exultation which I was sure he must feel. But this outburst of enthusiasm was too much even for Baxter, and it was clear that he was struggling with strong emotion when he rose to speak.

"Gentlemen, and fellow members of the Bodleian, it gives me unaffected pleasure—sincere pleasure—some day you may know how much pleasure—I cannot trust myself to say it now—to see the evident care with which your committee have read my poor verses, and the responsive sympathy with which my friends have entered into my views of life and conduct. I thank you again, and again, and when I say that I am too full for utterance—I'm sure you will excuse me from saying any more."

Baxter took his seat, and the applause had begun again when it was broken by a sudden exclamation.

"By Jove!" exclaimed our English visitor, who still sat behind the table, "what an extraordinary book!"

Everyone gathered around him.

"You see," he exclaimed, holding up the volume, "you fellows said so much about the bally book that I wanted to see what it was like; so I untied the ribbon and cut the leaves with the paper knife lying here and found—and found that there wasn't a single line in it, don't you know!"

Blank consternation followed this announcement, which proved only too true. Everyone knew instinctively, without further investigation, that the club had been badly sold. In the resulting confusion Baxter escaped, but later was waited upon by a committee, to whom he made the rather lame excuse that he had always regarded uncut and sealed books as tommy-rot, and that he had merely been curious to see how far the thing could go; and that the result had justified his belief that a book with nothing in it was just as useful to a book-collector as one embodying a work of genius. He offered to pay all the bills for the sham *Procrustes*, or to replace the blank copies with the real thing, as we might choose. Of course, after such an insult, the club did not care for the poem. He was permitted to pay the expense, however, and it was more than hinted to him that his resignation from the club would be favorably acted upon. He never sent it in, and, as he went to Europe shortly afterward, the affair had time to blow over.

In our first disgust at Baxter's duplicity, most of us cut our copies of the *Procrustes*, some of us mailed them to Baxter with cutting notes, and others threw them into the fire. A few wiser spirits held on to theirs, and this fact leaking out, it began to dawn upon the minds of the real collectors among us that the volume was something unique in the way of a publication.

"Baxter," said our president one evening to a select few of us who sat around the fireplace, "was wiser than we knew, or than he perhaps appreciated. His *Procrustes*, from the collector's point of view, is entirely logical, and might be considered as the acme of book-making. To the true collector, a book is a work of art, of which the contents are no more important than the words of an opera. Fine binding is a desideratum, and, for its cost, that of the *Procrustes* could not be improved upon. The paper is above criticism. The true collector loves wide margins, and the *Procrustes*, being all margin, merely touches the vanishing point of the perspective. The smaller the edition, the greater the collector's eagerness to acquire a copy. There are but six uncut copies left, I am told, of the *Procrustes*, and three sealed copies, of one of which I am the fortunate possessor."

After this deliverance, it is not surprising that, at our next auction, a sealed copy of Baxter's *Procrustes* was knocked down, after spirited bidding, for two hundred and fifty dollars, the highest price ever brought by a single volume published by the club.

THE DOLL

WHEN TOM Taylor, proprietor of the Wyandot Hotel barber shop, was leaving home, after his noonday luncheon, to return to his work, his daughter, a sprightly, diminutive brown maid, with very bright black eyes and very curly black hair, thrust into his coat pocket a little jointed doll somewhat the worse for wear.

"Now, don't forget, papa," she said in her shrill childish treble, "what's to be done to her. Her arms won't work, and her legs won't work, and she can't hold her head up. Be sure and have her mended this afternoon, and bring her home when you come to supper; for she's afraid of the dark, and always sleeps with me. I'll meet you at the corner at half-past six—and don't forget, whatever you do."

"No, Daisy, I'll not forget," he replied as he lifted her to the level of his lips and kissed her.

Upon reaching the shop he removed the doll from his pocket and hung it on one of the gilded spikes projecting above the wire netting surrounding the cashier's desk, where it would catch his eye. Some time during the afternoon he would send it to a toy shop around the corner for repairs. But the day was a busy one, and when the afternoon was well advanced he had not yet attended to it.

Colonel Forsyth had come up from the South to attend a conference of Democratic leaders to consider presidential candidates and platforms. He had put up at the Wyandot Hotel, but had been mainly in the hands of Judge Beeman, chairman of the local Jackson club, who was charged with the duty of seeing that the colonel was made comfortable and given the freedom of the city. It was after a committee meeting, and about four in the afternoon, that the two together entered the lobby of the Wyandot. They were discussing the platforms to be put forward by the two great parties in the approaching campaign.

"I reckon, judge," the colonel was saying, "that the Republican party will make a mistake if it injects the negro question into its platform.

109

The question is primarily a local one, and if the North will only be considerate about the matter, and let us alone, we can settle it to our entire satisfaction. The negro's place is defined by nature, and in the South he knows it and gives us no trouble."

"The Northern negroes are different," returned the judge.

"They are just the same," rejoined the colonel. "It is you who are different. You pamper them and they take liberties with you. But they are all from the South, and when they meet a Southerner they act accordingly. They are born to serve and to submit. If they had been worthy of equality they would never have endured slavery. They have no proper self-respect; they will neither resent an insult, nor defend a right, nor avenge a wrong."

"Well, now, colonel, aren't you rather hard on them? Consider their past."

"Hard? Why, no, bless your heart! I've got nothing against the nigger. I like him—in his place. But what I say is the truth. Are you in a hurry?"

"Not at all."

"Then come downstairs to the barber shop and I'll prove what I say."

The shop was the handsomest barber shop in the city. It was in the basement, and the paneled ceiling glowed with electric lights. The floor was of white tile, the walls lined with large mirrors. Behind ten chairs, of the latest and most comfortable design, stood as many colored barbers, in immaculate white jackets, each at work upon a white patron. An air of discipline and good order pervaded the establishment. There was no loud talking by patrons, no unseemly garrulity on the part of the barbers. It was very obviously a well-conducted barber shop, frequented by gentlemen who could afford to pay liberally for superior service. As the judge and the colonel entered, a customer vacated the chair served by the proprietor.

"Next gentleman," said the barber.

The colonel removed his collar and took his seat in the vacant chair, remarking, as he ran his hand over his neck, "I want a close shave, barber."

"Yes, sir; a close shave."

The barber was apparently about forty, with a brown complexion, clean-cut features and curly hair. Committed by circumstances to a career of personal service, he had lifted it by intelligence, tact and industry to the dignity of a successful business. The judge, a regular patron of the shop, knew him well and had often, while in his chair, conversed with him concerning his race—a fruitful theme, much on the public tongue.

"As I was saying," said the colonel, while the barber adjusted a towel about his neck, "the negro question is a perfectly simple one."

The judge thought it hardly good taste in the colonel to continue in his former strain. Northern men might speak slightingly of the negro, but seldom in his presence. He tried a little diversion.

"The tariff," he observed, "is a difficult problem."

"Much more complicated, suh, than the negro problem, which is perfectly simple. Let the white man once impress the negro with his superiority; let the negro see that there is no escape from the inevitable, and that ends it. The best thing about the negro is that, with all his limitations, he can recognize a finality. It is the secret of his persistence among us. He has acquired the faculty of evolution, suh—by the law of the survival of the fittest. Long ago, when a young man, I killed a nigger to teach him his place. One who learns a lesson of that sort certainly never offends again, nor fathers any others of his breed."

The barber, having lathered the colonel's face, was stropping his razor with long, steady strokes. Every word uttered by the colonel was perfectly audible to him, but his impassive countenance betrayed no interest. The colonel seemed as unconscious of the barber's presence as the barber of the colonel's utterance. Surely, thought the judge, if such freedom of speech were the rule in the South the colonel's contention must be correct, and the negroes thoroughly cowed. To a Northern man the situation was hardly comfortable.

"The iron and sugar interests of the South," persisted the judge, "will resist any reduction of the tariff."

The colonel was not to be swerved from the subject, nor from his purpose, whatever it might be.

"Quite likely they will; and we must argue with them, for they are white men and amenable to reason. The nigger, on the other hand, is the creature of instinct; you cannot argue with him; you must order him, and if he resists shoot him, as I did.

"Don't forget, barber," said the colonel, "that I want a close shave."

"No, sir," responded the barber, who having sharpened his razor, now began to pass it, with firm and even hand, over the colonel's cheek.

"It must have been," said the judge, "an aggravated case, to justify so extreme a step."

"Extreme, suh? I beg yo' pardon, suh, but I can't say I had regarded my conduct in that light. But it was an extreme case so far as the nigger was concerned. I am not boasting about my course; it was simply a disagreeable necessity. I am naturally a kind-hearted man, and don't like to kill even a fly. It was after the war, suh, and just as the Reconstruction period was drawing to a close. My mother employed a negro girl, the child of a former servant of hers, to wait upon her."

The barber was studying the colonel's face as the razor passed over his cheek. The colonel's eyes were closed, or he might have observed the sudden gleam of interest that broke through the barber's mask of self-effacement, like a flash of lightning from a clouded sky. Involuntarily the razor remained poised in midair, but, in less time than it takes to say it, was moving again, swiftly and smoothly, over the colonel's face. To shave a talking man required a high degree of skill, but they were both adept, each in his own trade—the barber at shaving, the colonel at talking.

"The girl was guilty of some misconduct, and my mother reprimanded her and sent her home. She complained to her father, and he came to see my mother about it. He was insolent, offensive and threatening. I came into the room and ordered him to leave it. Instead of obeying, he turned on me in a rage, suh, and threatened me. I drew my revolver and shot him. The result was unfortunate; but he and his people learned a lesson. We had no further trouble with bumptious niggers in our town."

"And did you have no trouble in the matter?" asked the judge.

"None, suh, to speak of. There were proceedings, but they were the merest formality. Upon my statement, confirmed by that of my mother, I was discharged by the examining magistrate, and the case was never even reported to the grand jury. It was a clear case of self-defense."

The barber had heard the same story, with some details ignored or forgotten by the colonel. It was the barber's father who had died at the colonel's hand, and for many long years the son had dreamed of this meeting.

He remembered the story in this wise: His father had been a slave. Freed by the Civil War, he had entered upon the new life with the zeal and enthusiasm of his people at the dawn of liberty, which seem, in the light of later discouragements, so pathetic in the retrospect. The chattel aspired to own property; the slave, forbidden learning, to educate his children. He had worked early and late, had saved his money with a thrift equal to that of a German immigrant and had sent his children regularly to school.

The girl—the barber remembered her very well—had been fair of feature, soft of speech and gentle of manner, a pearl among pebbles. One day her father's old mistress had met him on the street and, after a kindly inquiry about his family, had asked if she might hire his daughter during the summer, when there was no school. Her own married daughter would be visiting her, with a young child, and they wanted some neat and careful girl to nurse the infant.

"Why, yas m'am," the barber's father had replied. "I reckon it might be a good thing fer Alice. I wants her ter be a teacher; but she kin l'arn things from you, m'am, that no teacher kin teach her. She kin l'arn manners, m'am, an' white folks' ways, and nowhere better than in yo' house."

So Alice had gone to the home of her father's former mistress to learn white folks' ways. The lady had been kind and gracious. But there are ways and ways among all people.

When she had been three weeks in her new employment her mistress's son—a younger brother of the colonel—came home from college. Some weeks later Alice went home to her father. Who was most at fault the barber never knew. A few hours afterward the father called upon the lady. There was a stormy interview. Things were said to which the ears of white ladies were unaccustomed from the lips of black men. The elder son had entered the room and interfered. The barber's father had turned to him and exclaimed angrily:

"Go 'way from here, boy, and don't talk ter me, or I'm liable ter harm you."

The young man stood his ground. The negro advanced menacingly toward him. The young man drew his ready weapon and fatally wounded the negro—he lived only long enough, after being taken home, to gasp out the facts to his wife and children.

The rest of the story had been much as the colonel had related it. As the barber recalled it, however, the lady had not been called to testify, but was ill at the time of the hearing, presumably from the nervous shock.

That she had secretly offered to help the family the barber knew, and that her help had been rejected with cold hostility. He knew that the murderer went unpunished, and that in later years he had gone into politics, and became the leader and mouthpiece of his party. All the world knew that he had ridden into power on his hostility to negro rights.

The barber had been a mere boy at the time of his father's death, but not too young to appreciate the calamity that had befallen the household. The family was broke up. The sordid details of its misfortunes would not be interesting. Poverty, disease and death had followed them, until he alone was left. Many years had passed. The brown boy who had wept beside his father's bier, and who had never forgotten nor forgiven, was now the grave-faced, keen-eyed, deft-handed barber, who held a deadly weapon at the throat of his father's slayer.

How often he had longed for this hour! In his dreams he had killed this man a hundred times, in a dozen ways. Once, when a young man, he had gone to meet him, with the definite purpose of taking his life, but chance had kept them apart. He had imagined situations where they might come face to face; he would see the white man struggling in the water; he would have only to stretch forth his hand to save him; but he would tell him of his hatred and let him drown. He would see him in a burning house, from which he might rescue him; and he would call him murderer and let him burn! He would see him in the dock for murder of a white man, and only his testimony could save him, and he would let him suffer the fate that he doubly deserved! He saw a vision of his father's form, only an hour before thrilling with hope and energy, now stiff and cold in death; while under his keen razor lay the neck of his enemy, the enemy, too, of his race, sworn to degrade them, to teach them, if need be, with the torch and with the gun, that their place was at the white man's feet, his heel upon their neck; who held them in such contempt that he could speak as he had spoken in the presence of one of them. One stroke of the keen blade, a deflection of half an inch in its course, and a murder would be avenged, an enemy destroyed!

For the next sixty seconds the barber heard every beat of his own pulse, and the colonel, in serene unconsciousness, was nearer death than he had ever been in the course of a long and eventful life. He was only a militia colonel, and had never been under fire, but his turbulent political career had been passed in a community where life was lightly valued, where hot words were often followed by rash deeds, and murder was tolerated as a means of private vengeance and political advancement. He went on talking, but neither the judge nor the barber listened, each being absorbed in his own thoughts.

To the judge, who lived in a community where negroes voted, the colonel's frankness was a curious revelation. His language was choice, though delivered with the Southern intonation, his tone easy and conversational, and, addressing the barber directly, his manner had been courteous enough. The judge was interested, too, in watching the barber, who, it was evident, was repressing some powerful emotion. It seemed very probable to the judge that the barber might resent this cool recital of murder and outrage. He did not know what might be true of the negroes in the South, but he had been judge of a police court in one period of his upward career, and had found colored people prone to sudden rages, when under the influence of strong emotion, handy with edged tools, and apt to cut thick and deep, nor always careful about the color of the cuticle. The barber's feelings were plainly stirred, and the judge, a student of human nature, was curious to see if he would be moved to utterance. It would have been no novelty— patrons of the shop often discussed race questions with the barber. It was evident that the colonel was trying an experiment to demonstrate his contention in the lobby above. But the judge could not know the barber's intimate relation to the story, nor did it occur to him that the barber might conceive any deadly purpose because of a purely impersonal grievance. The barber's hand did not even tremble.

In the barber's mind, however, the whirlwind of emotions had passed lightly over the general and settled upon the particular injury. So strong, for the moment, was the homicidal impulse that it would have prevailed already had not the noisy opening of the door to admit a patron diverted the barber's attention and set in motion a current of ideas which fought for the colonel's life. The barber's glance toward the door, from force of habit, took in the whole shop. It was a handsome shop, and had been to the barber a matter of more than merely personal pride. Prominent among a struggling people, as yet scarcely beyond the threshold of citizenship, he had long been looked upon, and had become accustomed to regard himself, as a representative man, by whose failure or success his race would be tested. Should he slay this man now beneath his hand, this beautiful shop would be lost to his people. Years before the whole trade had been theirs. One by one the colored master barbers, trained in the slovenly old ways, had been forced to the wall by white competition, until his shop was one of the few good ones remaining in the hands of men of his race. Many an envious eye had been cast upon it. The lease had only a year to run. Strong pressure, he knew, had been exerted by a white rival to secure the reversion. The barber had the hotel proprietor's promise of a renewal; but he knew full well that should he lose the shop no colored man would succeed him; a center of industry, a medium of friendly contact with white men, would be lost to his people—many a good turn had the barber been able to do for them while he had the ear— literally had the ear—of some influential citizen, or held some aspirant for public office by the throat. Of the ten barbers in the shop all but one were married, with families dependent upon them for support. One was sending a son to college; another was buying a home. The unmarried one was in his spare hours studying a profession, with the hope of returning to practice it among his people in a Southern state. Their fates were all, in a measure, dependent upon the proprietor of the shop. Should he yield to the impulse which was swaying him, their livelihood would be placed in jeopardy. For what white man, while the memory of this tragic event should last, would trust his throat again beneath a negro's razor?

Such, however, was the strength of the impulse against which the barber was struggling that these considerations seemed likely not to prevail. Indeed, they had presented themselves to the barber's mind in a vague, remote, detached manner, while the dominant idea was present and compelling, clutching at his heart, drawing his arm, guiding his fingers. It was by their mass rather than by their clearness that these restraining forces held the barber's arm so long in check—it was society against self, civilization against the primitive instinct, typifying, more fully than the barber could realize, the great social problem involved in the future of his race.

He had now gone once over the colonel's face, subjecting that gentleman to less discomfort than he had for a long time endured while undergoing a similar operation. Already he had retouched one cheek and had turned the colonel's head to finish the other. A few strokes more and the colonel could be released with a close shave—how close he would never know!—or, one stroke, properly directed, and he would never stand erect again! Only the day before, the barber had read, in the newspapers, the account of a ghastly lynching in a Southern state, where, to avenge a single provoked murder, eight negroes had bit the dust and a woman had been burned at the stake for no other crime than that she was her husband's wife. One stroke and there would be one less of those who thus wantonly played with human life!

The uplifted hand had begun the deadly downward movement—when one of the barbers dropped a shaving cup, which was smashed to pieces on the marble floor. Fate surely fought for the colonel—or was it for the barber? Involuntarily the latter stayed his hand—instinctively his glance went toward the scene of the accident. It was returning to the upraised steel, and its uncompleted task, when it was arrested by Daisy's doll, hanging upon the gilded spike where he had left it.

If the razor went to its goal he would not be able to fulfill his promise to Daisy! She would wait for him at the corner, and wait in vain! If he killed the colonel he himself could hardly escape, for he was black and not white, and this was North and not South, and personal vengeance was not accepted by the courts as a justification for murder. Whether he died or not, he would be lost to Daisy. His wife was dead, and there would be no one to take care of Daisy. His own father had died in defense of his daughter; he must live to protect his own. If there was a righteous God, who divided the evil from the good, the colonel would some time get his just deserts. Vengeance was God's; it must be left to Him to repay!

The jointed doll had saved the colonel's life. Whether society had conquered self or not may be an open question, but it had stayed the barber's hand until love could triumph over hate!

The barber laid aside the razor, sponged off the colonel's face, brought him, with a movement of the chair, to a sitting posture, brushed his hair, pulled away the cloths from around his neck, handed him a pasteboard check for the amount of his bill, and stood rigidly by his chair. The colonel adjusted his collar, threw down a coin equal to double the amount of his bill and, without waiting for the change, turned with the judge to leave the shop. They had scarcely reached the door leading into the hotel lobby when the barber, overwrought by the long strain, collapsed heavily into the nearest chair.

"Well, judge," said the colonel, as they entered the lobby, "that was a good shave. What a sin it would be to spoil such a barber by making him a postmaster! I didn't say anything to him, for it don't do to praise a nigger much—it's likely to give him the big head—but I never had," he went on, running his hand appreciatively over his cheek, "I never had a better shave in my life. And I proved my theory. The barber is the son of the nigger I shot."

The judge was not sure that the colonel had proved his theory, and was less so after he had talked, a week later, with the barber. And, although the colonel remained at the Wyandot for several days, he did not get shaved again in the hotel barber shop.

DOVER·THRIFT·EDITIONS

NONFICTION

NARRATIVE OF THE LIFE OF FREDERICK DOUGLASS, Frederick Douglass. 96pp. 28499-9

SELF-RELIANCE AND OTHER ESSAYS, Ralph Waldo Emerson. 128pp. 27790-9

THE LIFE OF OLAUDAH EQUIANO, OR GUSTAVUS VASSA, THE AFRICAN, Olaudah Equiano. 192pp. 40661-X

THE AUTOBIOGRAPHY OF BENJAMIN FRANKLIN, Benjamin Franklin. 144pp. 29073-5

TOTEM AND TABOO, Sigmund Freud. 176pp. (Not available in Europe or United Kingdom.) 40434-X

LOVE: A Book of Quotations, Herb Galewitz (ed.). 64pp. 40004-2

PRAGMATISM, William James. 128pp. 28270-8

THE STORY OF MY LIFE, Helen Keller. 80pp. 29249-5

TAO TE CHING, Lao Tze. 112pp. 29792-6

GREAT SPEECHES, Abraham Lincoln. 112pp. 26872-1

THE PRINCE, Niccolò Machiavelli. 80pp. 27274-5

THE SUBJECTION OF WOMEN, John Stuart Mill. 112pp. 29601-6

SELECTED ESSAYS, Michel de Montaigne. 96pp. 29109-X

UTOPIA, Sir Thomas More. 96pp. 29583-4

BEYOND GOOD AND EVIL: Prelude to a Philosophy of the Future, Friedrich Nietzsche. 176pp. 29868-X

THE BIRTH OF TRAGEDY, Friedrich Nietzsche. 96pp. 28515-4

COMMON SENSE, Thomas Paine. 64pp. 29602-4

SYMPOSIUM AND PHAEDRUS, Plato. 96pp. 27798-4

THE TRIAL AND DEATH OF SOCRATES: Four Dialogues, Plato. 128pp. 27066-1

A MODEST PROPOSAL AND OTHER SATIRICAL WORKS, Jonathan Swift. 64pp. 28759-9

CIVIL DISOBEDIENCE AND OTHER ESSAYS, Henry David Thoreau. 96pp. 27563-9

SELECTIONS FROM THE JOURNALS (Edited by Walter Harding), Henry David Thoreau. 96pp. 28760-2

WALDEN; OR, LIFE IN THE WOODS, Henry David Thoreau. 224pp. 28495-6

NARRATIVE OF SOJOURNER TRUTH, Sojourner Truth. 80pp. 29899-X

THE THEORY OF THE LEISURE CLASS, Thorstein Veblen. 256pp. 28062-4

DE PROFUNDIS, Oscar Wilde. 64pp. 29308-4

OSCAR WILDE'S WIT AND WISDOM: A Book of Quotations, Oscar Wilde. 64pp. 40146-4

UP FROM SLAVERY, Booker T. Washington. 160pp. 28738-6

A VINDICATION OF THE RIGHTS OF WOMAN, Mary Wollstonecraft. 224pp. 29036-0

PLAYS

PROMETHEUS BOUND, Aeschylus. 64pp. 28762-9

THE ORESTEIA TRILOGY: Agamemnon, The Libation-Bearers and The Furies, Aeschylus. 160pp. 29242-8

LYSISTRATA, Aristophanes. 64pp. 28225-2

WHAT EVERY WOMAN KNOWS, James Barrie. 80pp. (Not available in Europe or United Kingdom.) 29578-8

THE CHERRY ORCHARD, Anton Chekhov. 64pp. 26682-6

THE SEA GULL, Anton Chekhov. 64pp. 40656-3

THE THREE SISTERS, Anton Chekhov. 64pp. 27544-2

UNCLE VANYA, Anton Chekhov. 64pp. 40159-6

THE WAY OF THE WORLD, William Congreve. 80pp. 27787-9

BACCHAE, Euripides. 64pp. 29580-X

MEDEA, Euripides. 64pp. 27548-5

DOVER·THRIFT·EDITIONS

FICTION

THE QUEEN OF SPADES AND OTHER STORIES, Alexander Pushkin. 128pp. 28054-3

THE STORY OF AN AFRICAN FARM, Olive Schreiner. 256pp. 40165-0

FRANKENSTEIN, Mary Shelley. 176pp. 28211-2

THE JUNGLE, Upton Sinclair. 320pp. (Available in U.S. only.) 41923-1

THREE LIVES, Gertrude Stein. 176pp. (Available in U.S. only.) 28059-4

THE BODY SNATCHER AND OTHER TALES, Robert Louis Stevenson. 80pp. 41924-X

THE STRANGE CASE OF DR. JEKYLL AND MR. HYDE, Robert Louis Stevenson. 64pp. 26688-5

TREASURE ISLAND, Robert Louis Stevenson. 160pp. 27559-0

GULLIVER'S TRAVELS, Jonathan Swift. 240pp. 29273-8

THE KREUTZER SONATA AND OTHER SHORT STORIES, Leo Tolstoy. 144pp. 27805-0

THE WARDEN, Anthony Trollope. 176pp. 40076-X

FIRST LOVE AND DIARY OF A SUPERFLUOUS MAN, Ivan Turgenev. 96pp. 28775-0

FATHERS AND SONS, Ivan Turgenev. 176pp. 40073-5

ADVENTURES OF HUCKLEBERRY FINN, Mark Twain. 224pp. 28061-6

THE ADVENTURES OF TOM SAWYER, Mark Twain. 192pp. 40077-8

THE MYSTERIOUS STRANGER AND OTHER STORIES, Mark Twain. 128pp. 27069-6

HUMOROUS STORIES AND SKETCHES, Mark Twain. 80pp. 29279-7

AROUND THE WORLD IN EIGHTY DAYS, Jules Verne. 160pp. 41111-7

CANDIDE, Voltaire (François-Marie Arouet). 112pp. 26689-3

GREAT SHORT STORIES BY AMERICAN WOMEN, Candace Ward (ed.). 192pp. 28776-9

"THE COUNTRY OF THE BLIND" AND OTHER SCIENCE-FICTION STORIES, H. G. Wells. 160pp. (Not available in Europe or United Kingdom.) 29569-9

THE ISLAND OF DR. MOREAU, H. G. Wells. 112pp. (Not available in Europe or United Kingdom.) 29027-1

THE INVISIBLE MAN, H. G. Wells. 112pp. (Not available in Europe or United Kingdom.) 27071-8

THE TIME MACHINE, H. G. Wells. 80pp. (Not available in Europe or United Kingdom.) 28472-7

THE WAR OF THE WORLDS, H. G. Wells. 160pp. (Not available in Europe or United Kingdom.) 29506-0

ETHAN FROME, Edith Wharton. 96pp. 26690-7

SHORT STORIES, Edith Wharton. 128pp. 28235-X

THE AGE OF INNOCENCE, Edith Wharton. 288pp. 29803-5

THE PICTURE OF DORIAN GRAY, Oscar Wilde. 192pp. 27807-7

JACOB'S ROOM, Virginia Woolf. 144pp. (Not available in Europe or United Kingdom.) 40109-X